ECHOES OF ANCIENT DREAMS

A Time Travel/Ancient Celtic Novella

By Kathryn Le Veque

2

Printed by Dragonblade Publishing in the United States of America

Other Novels by Kathryn Le Veque

Medieval Romance:

The White Lord of Wellesbourne
The Dark One: Dark Knight

While Angels Slept
Rise of the Defender
Spectre of the Sword
Unending Love
Archangel
Lord of the Shadows

Great Protector
To the Lady Born

The Falls of Erith
Lord of War: Black Angel

The Darkland
Black Sword

Unrelated characters or family groups:
The Whispering Night
The Dark Lord
The Gorgon
The Warrior Poet
Guardian of Darkness (related to The Fallen One)
Tender is the Knight
The Legend
Lespada
The Wolfe
Lord of Light

The Dragonblade Trilogy:
Dragonblade
Island of Glass
The Savage Curtain
The Fallen One
Fragments of Grace

Novella, Time Travel Romance:
Echoes of Ancient Dreams

Time-Travel Romance:
The Crusader
Kingdom Come

Contemporary Romance:

Kathlyn Trent/Marcus Burton Series:
Valley of the Shadow
The Eden Factor
Canyon of the Sphinx

The American Heroes Series:
Resurrection
Fires of Autumn
Evenshade
Sea of Dreams
Purgatory

Other Contemporary Romance:
Lady of Heaven
Darkling, I listen

Note: All Kathryn's novels are designed to be read as stand-alones, although many have cross-over characters or cross-over family groups.

Novels that are grouped together have related characters or family groups.

Series are clearly marked. All series contain the same characters or family groups except the American Heroes Series, which is an anthology with unrelated characters.

There is NO particular chronological order for any of the novels because they can all be read as stand-alones, even the series.

6

CHAPTER ONE

"What in the hell is *that* guy doing up there?"

The woman asking the question looked genuinely curious. Her friend, wrapped up against the cold late afternoon temperature and kicking at a rock in the middle of the footpath, glanced up to see what the woman was referring to.   She could see a man at the top of the green, damp mound, a very big man, speaking with great animation to a group of young people.

"That guy?" she pointed.

"Yes," he friend nodded. "He's waving his arms around like he's trying to take off."

The friend giggled, looking back to the footpath they were on so she wouldn't trip. "I have no idea," she snorted. "These ancient religious places affected people. "

The woman looked around; it was a beautiful afternoon in the lush countryside of Ireland, a color of green she had never seen before. It was so vibrant that it was almost neon in patches. The weather was cool and damp, as it had rained heavily that morning, but now the sun was out and everything just seemed fresh and vivid. A cool breeze blew in from the Irish Sea to the east, stirring the bushes and branches as they walked up the path towards the animated man and his captive audience.

"It's not just these religious sites," the woman shoved her hands deep into the pockets of her jacket as the wind picked up. "It's the Irish in general."

The friend turned to look at her. "Don't bash my people."

The woman struggled not to giggle. "They're my people, too. I can bash them if I want to."

The friend burst out in soft laughter. "You're an Irish racist, Destry."

Destry Caldbeck joined the laughter, her straight teeth white and gleaming. "How can I be a racist against my own race?" she wanted to know. "I'm just stating a fact; all Irish are crazy."

The two women snorted and giggled as they made their way up the muddy, grassy path to the great Neolithic burial mound of Dowth. About thirty-two miles north of Dublin, it was a massive Neolithic site that was larger than its better known counterpart, New Grange. Not many people came to visit Dowth, but Destry and her friend Aisling had made the trip, mostly because Aisling was kicking Destry all the way across Ireland and forcing her to participate in activities when Destry would rather be sitting in a pub drowning her sorrows. A broken engagement had that effect on her.

Now Aisling and Destry were enjoying what should have been Destry's honeymoon, but it had been an uphill battle. Distraction and constant sightseeing had been Aisling's way of handling it. Even now, she tried to keep the mood light as they reached the crest of the ancient mound, noting the enormous man with the group around him at closer range. The man was indeed waving his arms around, jumping up and down and apparently acting out some kind of scene as the people around him watched intently. Aisling and Destry couldn't help but watch him, too, until Destry finally shook her head and looked away. She pulled a small guidebook out of her pocked and began to read.

"Okay," she sighed, finding her place in the book. "Let's see what this has to say; Dowth dates from around three thousand B.C. and has all sorts of underground storage chambers. It's part of the Brú na Bóinne monuments."

Aisling looked around the top of the mound where they were standing. "What does that mean?"

Destry continued to read. "Neolithic monuments like New Grange."

"That one is next on our list."

"I know." Destry put the guidebook down and began to look around. "This is really big."

Aisling began to wander. "Huge," she agreed, wrapping her scarf more tightly about her neck. "Why is it so darn cold? You would think it was January and not September. I feel like I'm in the Arctic."

Destry shrugged. "Maybe we should have gone to the Bahamas."

"Maybe."

Aisling continued wandering, looking at their surroundings. Then she suddenly came to a halt, cocking her head in the direction of the man and his group. She listened a moment before looking to Destry.

"It sounds like he's giving a tour." She was trying not to yell as she pointed. "I can hear him."

Destry's bright blue eyes lingered on the man several dozen feet away. "Should we go listen?"

Aisling wriggled her eyebrows devilishly. "We didn't pay for the tour. Not only that, but we busted through the fence to get up here. I really don't think we're even supposed to be here."

Destry shrugged. "So what?" she said. "The worst he can do is tell us to go away."

Aisling giggled as Destry began to saunter casually in the direction of the group. The area of the top of the mound was fairly vast and uneven, and had been closed off to the public. But Destry and Aisling had climbed through the fence anyway and walked up the narrow path. As they neared the group, they could hear the man as he continued his story.

"…tomb was emptied of its original contents when it was plundered by Viking raiders around 861 A.D., who basically plundered all of the tombs in the Boyne Valley," he was saying with great drama. "Much of our Irish heritage ended up on a long boat bound for Scandinavia, where some of it is now in Scandinavian museums."

A young college student with a dirty stocking cap on his head threw up a hand and began to speak. "Dr. Daderga?" he called. "Haven't we tried to get our treasures back from the Scandinavians?"

Dr. Conor Daderga turned to look at the young man with a wry smirk on his face. "It's like the British stealing treasures from Egypt and putting them in the British Museum," he said, his Irish brogue extremely heavy and dramatic to the point of barely being understandable. "The Limeys won't give them back to Egypt and the Viking plunderers won't give us back our treasures, either. They stole our history and claim it as their own."

A question and answer session followed as Destry and Aisling stood at the back of the group, listening; Destry's attention was mostly on the teacher and not on the students. Since the group was made up of young adults, she could only assume it was a college class. Dr. Daderga was, in fact, everything an Irishman should be; he was loud, passionate, animated, handsome, and had a deep red mustache and goatee that stood out against his milky –white skin. Even though the man was bundled up against the cold, she could see that he had very red hair beneath his well-worn newsboy cap.

But she noticed more; he was absolutely enormous in both size and height; at three inches over five feet, the man had to be well over a foot taller than she was and he was built like a linebacker. She thought he was very good-looking with his chiseled features and brilliant smile, something that Aisling silently agreed with as she flashed a wicked smile in Destry's direction.

And he was dynamic, too. Great passion came forth as he moved away from plundered Irish history and began to describe the history of Dowth. He waved his arms and bugged his eyes as he described ancient man and their toils on the mound. Then he began to speak of more recent history, of the Dark Age village that had popped up around Dowth, fragments of which had been excavated.

Destry watched the man, finding herself focusing more on his handsome features than what he was actually saying. A couple of times, their eyes met and she felt strangely unsettled as he focused in on her. The man had intense blue eyes, bordering on something charismatic and powerful, and Destry was too fragile to rationally deal with anything intensely male at the moment. She tried to stay and listen but his gaze kept coming back to her, each look more potent than the last. Disturbed, she broke off from the group as Aisling remained to listen, and wandered away.

The grass was thick, wet and vibrantly green as she made her way down the side of the mound. She lost her footing a couple of times and slid in the grass, eventually ending up at the bottom of the mound.

It was heavily wooded around the base of the mound, thick brush and trees growing out from the sides. She pulled out her guidebook and began to read again, noting that the guidebook said there were three entrances at the base of the mound, all facing southwest. Getting her bearings, she shifted direction and wandered through the brush and trees until she came to the first of the three passages.

The first passage was small and all she could see was darkness beyond the stone-braced doorway. There weren't any barriers but she didn't feel like charging in to a bottomless black pit. Moreover, she didn't have a flashlight and the sun was beginning to set, so it was difficult to see more than just a few feet inside. But she could smell wet earth and mold coming forth, invisible wisps of ancient times that were reaching out for her. She wasn't superstitious and she wasn't easily spooked, but something about the dark bowels of the ancient burial mound made her shiver. Maybe it was just the coldness of the air coming forth; whatever it was, she shrugged it off and moved to the next entrance.

She could see more through this entrance but it wasn't any grander than the last. It was just old and creepy. Moving on to the third entrance, she moved in and out of the heavy growth, trying not to get wet from the moisture that still lingered. Over to the southwest, the sun was sitting on the horizon as night began to approach and Destry was beginning to think that they should head back to the car shortly. She was looking forward to a hot meal and a hot bath, in that order. Maybe they would also hit a few of the pubs, seeking some solace and distraction in the Irish past time. Not that she wanted to get drunk. Well, maybe. It seemed to be the only thing that made her forget about the hell of the past two weeks.

The third passage was taller than the other two with the same black-hole entrance. Destry couldn't see more than a few feet inside of it, wishing she had brought a flashlight. She could feel the cold dampness from this hole reaching out to her again, caressing her face with cold velvet fingers. It also smelled strange, like the dank depths of a grave, which it essentially was. The guidebook said that medieval people used the mound to store food and that there was a storage chamber inside. Destry peered into the blackness, noticing the weak rays of the setting sun were shining on this side of the mound. A few rays streamed through the bushes and fell upon the peripheral of the ancient doorway. She stood a moment, hoping if she waited a few minutes that the sun would act as a flashlight and shine some rays down into the tunnel.

It was growing colder now as the sun was lowering and she tightened up her scarf and shoved her hands into her pockets, waiting for the sun to shine its dying rays into the ancient tunnel. The breeze had picked up, too, filtering through the bushes around her. The wind whipped into the passageway and found its way out again, whistling as it did so. The first couple of times, it whipped around her and she shivered against the cold. Then came a particularly strong gust of wind that soared through the ancient mound, into one of the other tunnels and then blasting out of the tunnel where Destry was standing. She turned her back on it as it swirled around her, chilling her, whistling through the stone and earth with an odd hum. At the height of the gust, she thought she heard something whispered upon the wind.

Startled, Destry turned to the ancient tunnel to see if someone was standing there. It sounded as if someone had whispered to her, a breathy gasp that was quickly gone. But the tunnel was dark, the wind brisk, and she shook her head, thinking she must be crazy for thinking she heard something. Maybe all of the travel and Guinness was getting to her. Yawning, she watched the sun set lower on the horizon, turning to see that some of the weak rays were nearly upon the tunnel. She was looking forward to seeing what was deep down inside the hill. But suddenly, another gust of wind whipped through the mound and she turned away from the tunnel as bits of rock and loose earth kicked up at her. Closing her eyes against the flying dust, the whisper on the wind filled her ears again.

"*Etain!*"

Destry jumped at the sound, turning back to the dark opening now that the sun was just beginning to fall upon it. She gazed at it suspiciously, curiously, almost angrily, thinking that someone was playing tricks on her.

"Hello?" she called. "Who's in there? Come out of there or I'm coming in."

Nothing but the wind answered. Level-headed and brutally practical, Destry waited for a few red-headed Irish kids to come running out to scare her. But no one emerged from the tunnel and just as she moved in to get a closer look, the sun's rays suddenly hit upon the ancient entrance, reflecting on stone and earth that had seen five hundred centuries of such events. The sun reached the rock, cut by the ancients, and the cold porous blocks roared to life.

Suddenly, it was very bright in the entrance and Destry could see all the way back to the end of the tunnel where it seemed to open up into blackness. The walls of the tunnel were lined with stone, great carved slabs that held back the tons of earth surrounding it. The sun gave the stone a strangely yellow glow, reflecting the brilliance of the setting rays. But as Destry studied the tunnel with interest and some awe, the yellow glow took on an even brighter countenance.

It wasn't so much the stone as something else seemed to be creating a light of its own. The great yellow glow became brighter and brighter until it was nearly white. Destry put a hand up to shield the glare from her eyes and as she did so, something in the midst of the great white glow reached towards her.

"Etain!"

It wasn't one whisper; it was several. It was like hundreds of children whispering as one, a chorus of angels that breathed life upon the earth. Destry felt a great rush of air as the whisper burst forth like a thousand shooting stars, reaching out to touch her. It all happened so fast that she didn't have time to be startled; as she stood there with her hand raised, something brushed against her hand and she heard the chorus of whispers once more.

"Fanacht, morrigan, gnáthlá agus oiche og ceanna; tar ar cúl do sinne."

Destry didn't even remember running away until she was halfway up the hill. Her heart was pounding and her head swimming, so frightened that she could hardly think straight. But suddenly, she was walking very quickly up the hill, anxious to put space in between her and the mysterious tunnel. She had no idea what it was, those odd whispers, but the touch had sent her scurrying. She had a difficult time processing the experience as she struggled up the slippery grass.

 For several long moments, disorientation consumed her. There was no way that whatever happened was real, she told herself firmly. She forced herself to calm, taking deep breaths, struggling with her equilibrium and her composure. It hadn't been real; it couldn't have been. The sunlight, the wind, had been playing tricks on her.

She kept telling herself that, over and over. By the time she reached the top of the mound, she was slightly less frazzled, but only barely. At least she wasn't gasping for air any longer. Up on the crest of the mound, the students had disbanded and were walking around the ancient mound in small clusters, inspecting it, and she could see Aisling standing with the tall and imposing figure of Dr. Daderga. She was talking to him about something, her hands flying all around as they usually did when she talked.

Taking another deep breath, and with a hind glance over her shoulder, Destry made her way over to Aisling and Dr. Daderga. But she swore that the whispers were following.

CHAPTER TWO

Conor saw her coming.

He saw her the moment she crested the top of the hill, the very moment her gaze turned in his direction. He'd noticed her the first time she and her friend had joined his class, a woman of unearthly beauty and brilliant blue eyes. He couldn't seem to stop staring at her, like she was a magnet and his eyes were steel. The two kept coming together and he could feel the sparks fly every time. Something about that woman leapt out at him like nothing he had ever experienced before. It was a strange and alluring sensation, and one not easily discarded.

Her friend, a nice young lady with the good Irish name of Aisling, had engaged him in conversation when his class broke up. As his students went about on exploration before the sun sank too low, the young woman with curly brown hair and brown eyes had approached him with a smile. She had wanted to know if he had any information about the great burial mound at Knowth and whether or not the legends were true about it being a portal into the Underworld.

Conor had responded politely to her foolish question, mostly because she was American and he knew she was only repeating what she had heard or seen in movies. Most Americans viewed the world the way their movies portrayed it. But he was also courteous to her because of the fair skinned goddess that had accompanied her on the off-hand chance that he might actually get to speak with her.

She was heading right for him. His hopes were about to be fulfilled. He couldn't help but stare at the woman as she approached; she was short in stature, clad in sweaters and jeans, but there was no mistaking her curvy figure. Her light brown hair was long, with streaks of blond in it and cut into one of those layered styles that could be very sexy with a toss of the head. As the woman came upon them, he was struck by the pure porcelain beauty of her face and eyes so bright that they were nearly glowing. He'd never seen such a brilliant shade of blue. When their eyes finally met, he felt his heart flutter in his chest. He stared at her with a dumb grin on his face as Aisling spoke.

"Where did you wander off to?" she asked her friend.

The woman threw a thumb over her shoulder. "Down the hill," she said in a sweet, sultry voice. "There are passages down there."

"Passages?" Aisling was curious but remembered her manners, indicating the big Irishman standing next to her. "This is Dr. Daderga," she introduced him. "He's a professor over at Trinity College in Dublin. We apparently invaded his class."

The woman turned to him, her bright blue eyes swallowing him up. She extended a hand. "Nice to meet you, Dr. Daderga," she said. "Destry Caldbeck."

Conor was stupefied as he shook her soft, warm hand, feeling rather overwhelmed with such beauty. He felt like an idiot just staring at her and realized he should probably say something in return. *Where have you been all my life, gorgeous?*

"Nice to meet you," he replied in his heavy Irish accent. "You're American also?"

Destry nodded. "I am," she replied. "California."

"Where in California?"

"San Diego." She pulled her hand discreetly from his grip because he hadn't let her go yet. He just stood there holding her hand. There was something very big and virile and overwhelming about him. "Thank you for letting us infiltrate your class. You looked like you were having a lot of fun."

He smiled at her; in fact, he couldn't seem to stop smiling at her. "I was," he replied. "This is one of my Ancient Irish History classes; we've toured three of the major sites today, this one being our last. It's going to get dark quickly so they're taking a few moments to explore the site before we buzz off."

Destry nodded, glancing around at the students who were spread out over the top of the mound, poking around.

"You certainly had their attention with your stories," she said. "It sounds like you have a pretty cool class."

His grin grew. "They're not stories," he corrected her. "They're Irish history."

She laughed softly, displaying her beautiful smile and big dimple in her left cheek. "I believe you," she said. "In fact, it wouldn't hurt Aisling or me to learn a little Irish history. Aisling's parents were born in Ireland and my mother's parents were both born in Ireland before immigrating to the States back in the nineteen fifties. That's sort of why we're here; to get back in touch with our roots."

Conor was completely focused on Destry, the shape of her face and the soft curve of her lips. He couldn't seem to look at anything else. "Welcome back."

Destry grinned at him, giving him a quirky lift of the shoulder. "Thank you," she said. "It's good to be back."

He laughed softly, shoving his hands in his pockets as the wind picked up. "There's a problem, though."

"What?"

"You're lacking a good Irish name like your friend. I'm surprised they let you into the country."

In spite of herself, Destry was finding herself upswept in his charm. There was something very magnetic about him. "My middle name is Kenna," she offered, putting up her hand as if swearing in court. "I promise; my mother named me after my grandmother, so there really is Irish in me."

"Kenna," he rolled it off his tongue with his heavy Irish brogue. "It means ancient one. But I have no idea what Destry means."

"It's of French origin. It means desired."

He grinned from ear to ear. "Then I approve," he said. "It suits you perfectly."

Destry laughed, feeling rather giddy for a woman who had been wallowing in rejected misery for the past two weeks. Dr. Daderga's compliments were doing something to ease that great big hole where her heart had once been. In fact, his entire presence had an odd effect on her, making her feel light and happy like she hadn't felt in a very long time. She had seriously wondered over the past several days if she would ever be happy again.

"Thank you very much, Dr. Daderga," she said graciously, distracted when a big gust of wind suddenly whipped around her and reminded her of the bizarre experience she'd had a few moments before. She couldn't help but think of the whispers, of the word she heard more than once come from that dark and unnatural tunnel. Since Daderga seemed to be an expert on the site, she decided to probe him a little to see if she'd really been imagining things. "Do you mind giving us a crash course in this site? Anything interesting that the guidebook doesn't tell us?"

He looked around, watching his students wander around the slick, green hill. "It's a Neolithic burial mound," he said. "During the dark ages, the indigenous population used to say that the gods lived under mounds like this. It was their way of explaining away what Stone Age man had built."

Destry thought of the howling passage, of her experience, and began to get creeped out again.

"Have you ever heard the word 'Etain'?" she asked, out of the blue.

Conor turned to look at her. "Of course," he said. "She's a heroine in Irish mythology."

A bolt of shock ran through Destry and she glanced uneasily down the hill where the dark passages loomed. All of the effort she had taken to convince herself that the experience had been in her imagination was torpedoed by those eight little words.

"Seriously?" she asked, feeling somewhat sick. "It's a woman?"

"Absolutely."

Destry's sense of uneasiness increased. "Is she evil?" she asked, then quickly clarified because she didn't want him to think she was some oddball. "I mean, what was her story? Did she live underneath one of these mounds?"

He shook his head. "No," he replied. "She's a heroine in some of the earliest Irish Mythology cycles. She appears a few times in a few different stories. Why do you ask?"

There was no way Destry was going to tell him the reason behind her questions. She shook her head, almost too quickly.

"No reason," she replied. "Just curious. I heard the name somewhere and I was just... curious."

He bought her explanation, his gaze lingering on her. "I'd be happy to refer you to some books on Irish Mythology that recite Etain's tales. Or I could tell you the stories myself. Sometime. If you're not too busy."

The man didn't waste any time; he had known her all of two minutes and was already asking her on a date without really asking. As much as he had charmed her, Destry wasn't ready to visit with or otherwise interact with a man one on one, no matter how attracted she was to him. Too much about her personal life was painful and unsettled, and she didn't want to complicate things. Problem was, she couldn't bring herself to flatly turn him down.

"You know all of the Irish mythology stories by heart?" she asked with incredulity, somewhat shifting the subject.

He shrugged, grinning again. "It's my job to know them," he said. "Plus, they're very exciting. Better than the movies."

"I saw you reciting something to your students earlier, flapping your arms around. Were you telling them some of the stories?"

"Of course," his grin broadened. "What else would I be doing?"

A sharp whistle suddenly pierced the air and they turned to see one of the male students whistling to the group, rounding them up. Aisling, having been largely ignored throughout the conversation between Destry and Dr. Daderga, tugged on Destry's arm.

"Come on," she said. "It's getting dark and we need to head back. I'm not comfortable driving on the right side of the car on these small roads after dark."

Destry followed as Aisling began to walk, turning to thank Dr. Daderga for his time but seeing that he was trailing after them. Everyone was traveling in herds towards the slope that led down to the car park on the west side of the mound as the world around them began to dim with the coming night.

"How long are you both here?" Conor strolled up beside Destry. "Are you doing any tours or just winging it?"

Destry glanced up at the man. "We're here for another five days and then we head to Paris," she told him. "We took a tour yesterday in Dublin and tomorrow we're doing a tour of ancient religious sites on the outskirts of Dublin."

He nodded casually at the information as his students milled around and behind them, all trudging down to the car park.

"So you're staying in Dublin?" he asked.

She nodded. "We're staying at the O'Callaghan Davenport," she told him." It's by the National Gallery."

He bobbed his head quickly. "I know exactly where it is," he said. "You're not far from the college."

"I didn't know that."

He wriggled his eyebrows. "That's a fairly nice hotel. It's famous for its Honeymoon Suite, you know. It's supposed to be very romantic."

Destry was staring at the ground as she spoke. "It is," she said softly, then turned to look at him with a forced smile. "It was very nice to meet you, Dr. Daderga. Good luck with your class."

Conor watched her very quickly make her way down the footpath toward the darkening car park. Aisling was still walking a few feet away from him, her brown eyes focused sorrowfully on her friend. She cast an apologetic glance at Conor.

"Thanks again," she said politely. "It was very nice to meet you."

Before she could scoot after Destry, he reached out and stopped her.

"I'm sorry if I said something offensive," he said, his eyes lingering on Destry at the base of the mound. "I think I upset your friend. I didn't mean to."

Aisling gazed down the hill, watching Destry squeeze through the fence and head towards the car. It wasn't like they were ever going to see Daderga again so she just told him the truth.

"Don't worry about it," she said. "You didn't know. The O'Callaghan really does have a hell of a honeymoon suite and I was supposed to be her husband."

"Come again?"

"She supposed to be on her honeymoon right now. But I came instead of her groom."

Conor got it, sort of. He watched Aisling skip down the trail after Destry, watching the woman slide through the fence in pursuit of her friend. She was supposed to be on her honeymoon, he rolled the words over in his head. It was a sad tale but he couldn't honestly believe what idiot would refuse to marry that woman; she was absolutely perfect and then some.

While he felt a great deal of sympathy for her, the larger part of him was very glad that she didn't get married. He had her name and the place she was staying at. Right or wrong, like it or not, he intended to do something about it.

CHAPTER THREE

Conor got the shock of his life the next morning.

It was around six-thirty a.m., a full hour and a half before his eight o'clock class on Early Irish Gaelic. He had some papers to grade and some other work to attend to, so he had come in early.   The building his office was housed in was the West Theater, an old building on the campus of Trinity College that was well over one hundred years old. It was built of brick and solid masonry, able to withstand the test of time, and always smelled like moldy old stone.

Conor had his arms full of his briefcase, laptop and lunch bag as he entered his office suite. The door was unlocked and his secretary's desk empty; she didn't arrive for another hour. Even so, there was someone sitting in her office.

Destry stood up from the chair she had been patiently planted in as Conor entered the office. His gaze fell on her and he came to a halt, startled. The lunch bag fell to the ground and Destry bent down to retrieve it.

"Hi," she smiled weakly at him, propping the lunch bag back on top of his briefcase.

He stared at her a moment as if hardly believing what he was seeing. "Hi yourself," he replied, a baffled but delighted expression coming to his handsome features. "Uh... what are you doing here?"

Destry's weak smile became genuine. "That's a very good question," she said, suddenly putting her hands up. "Don't worry; I'm not stalking you."

His gaze lingered on her as he moved for his office door. "I'm disappointed," he teased. "Are you sure?"

She giggled. "Pretty sure."

"Can I talk you into it?"

Her laughter grew. "Probably not."

He opened his door. "Truly unfortunate," he said, bobbing is head in the direction of his now-open office. "Care to come in so we can discuss it further?"

Smirking, Destry preceded him into his office, standing near his cluttered desk as he dumped the contents in his arms onto the desktop. She watched him unload, noting he looked distinctly different than he had yesterday; the baseball cap had concealed flaming red hair which he had spiked this morning so that it was standing straight up in the air. It was the tallest flat-top she had ever seen, increasing his already substantial height.

Given his red goatee and mustache, he looked like a pirate. But his skin was beautiful and milky, and his eyes a clear blue. He was a unique-looking man but absolutely and powerfully handsome.

As he pulled off his jacket, he was wearing a worn collared shirt beneath and when the jacket came off completely, Destry's eyebrows lifted at the size of the man's arms and chest; she had noticed yesterday that he was a big boy but she had no idea just how big. The most obvious physical attribute was that he was exceptionally tall; he had to be at least six and a half feet in height. But he was also enormous in breadth, powerfully built like a weight lifter with a massive upper body and a chiseled torso. He also had very big legs – she could see them through the jeans he wore. The shirt he wore was rather form fitting in displaying his powerful physique. In fact, it made her a little hot to gaze at those beautifully massive biceps so she tried not to stare as she spoke.

"I'm really sorry to intrude on you so early," she said as he hung up his coat. "I was wondering if you could give me a couple of minutes of your time. I won't take long, I promise."

He turned around from the coat rack and faced her. "I can give you all the time you need until my eight o'clock class," he said. "How'd you find me, by the way?"

She shrugged. "You said you worked at Trinity College. I looked you up in the directory and followed the map."

He nodded faintly, eyeing the woman who only seemed to grow more beautiful with each passing second. Her hair was pulled into a ponytail, revealing the beautiful shape of her face, and she was dressed in a sweater and jeans that accentuated a figure he had only seen on the pages of men's magazines. The sweater she was wearing gave a tantalizing peek of spectacular cleavage but he tried not to let his eyes wander down there. He could have stared at that for the rest of his life. But as he looked at her face, he noticed that she looked exhausted. Her bright blue eyes were somewhat dim. Curious, he indicated the seat in front of his desk.

"Then I'm honored," he said as he took a seat; his old chair creaked and groaned under his considerable weight. "Are you here to take me up on my offer of telling you more glorious Celtic legends?"

Her weak smile returned and she glanced around his office; artwork of Celtic crosses lined the walls, as did replicas and images of swords and other battle instruments. There was also a great big cape that had some kind of Celtic knot sewn into it, matted to the biggest shadowbox she had ever seen. All in all, it was an office full of rich Celtic relics, something he displayed proudly as a man dedicated to the history of his people.

"Sort of," she replied to his question, suddenly looking uncomfortable. "I didn't know who else to ask about this."

He sat forward, folding his hands on his desk. His blue eyes were intense. "Ask what?"

Destry took a deep breath, trying to figure out how to start this conversation. She'd been trying to figure out how to start it for the past two hours, ever since she decided to seek out Dr. Daderga. She'd been up all night with the dilemma and now, she hardly knew where to begin. But she had to start somewhere. She could only hope she didn't come across like a madwoman.

"Okay, here goes," she puffed out her cheeks and fixed him in the eye. "Dr. Daderga, I know you don't know me but I want to assure you that I'm not an idiot or a drama queen. I'm actually quite normal; I have a master's degree in Nursing and I'm a shift supervisor in the coronary care unit at the University of San Diego Medical Center. I come from a nice, normal family with a mom and a dad and a younger sister. I don't drink and I don't do drugs. I was a cheerleader for the San Diego Chargers for a couple of years and I also do charity work, if that makes any difference. Anyway, I'm a normal girl. But I really need to ask you a question."

His dark blue gaze was glittering at her over the top of his desk. "Ask away. I'm all yours."

She stared at him a moment before finally shaking her head. "Please don't think I'm nuts, but I've been up all night with terrible nightmares. I haven't been able to sleep at all. Ever since I left that mound yesterday, I've been having all sorts of... well, crazy thoughts. Really crazy things."

He sat back in his chair. "Like what?"

She threw up her hands and he could see how exasperated she was, almost bordering on tears. "All night, every time I fell asleep, I'd have these dreams that I was back at the mound and people inside of it were talking to me."

His brow furrowed. "People *inside* of it?"

She nodded vigorously. "Yes," she insisted. "It was like they were ghosts or something, and I could hear them, like whispers. They kept trying to talk to me and reach out to me. But I couldn't understand what they were saying."

He was trying not to grin at her, thinking that her problem was more than likely just an overactive imagination. Ancient tales and an ancient site could do that to people who were not accustomed to such things. Personally, he didn't really care why she was here, crazy stories notwithstanding, because it gave him an excuse to see her again. He remained casual in his reply.

"So you've come to me to interpret your nightmares?" he said. "That's really not in my scope of work, but I'll give it a try. What did they say?"

Destry thought a moment, terrified that if she closed her eyes again to remember the words, then she would start having those visions again. They swamped her all night, faceless wraiths that invaded her dreams and whispered mysterious words to her. Even thinking about them again made her heart pound. She had been so scared that she had sat up most of the night in the bathroom with the light on. She just couldn't face the dark again. She gazed at Conor with some pain in her expression.

"I hope you can figure it out," she murmured sincerely, "because I've never had anything like this happen to me, ever, and you were the only person I could think of that might know."

"Like I said, I'll give it a go. What were the words?"

"I don't even know what language they were. They sounded like gibberish to me."

"More than likely, since it was a dream. Do you remember them?

She took a deep breath before haltingly spitting them out. "Fanacht, morrigan, gnáthlá agus oiche og ceanna; tar ar cúl do sinne."

Conor's smile vanished with unnatural rapidity. He stared at her, sitting forward in his chair as a queer expression crossed his features.

"What?" he said, as if he couldn't think of anything else to say. "Where did you hear that?"

She looked sick and scared. "I told you," she said wearily. "That's what those… those ghosts said to me in my dreams. Do you know what language it is? Is it even a language?"

The longer he looked at her, the more confused he became. He suddenly stood up, moving his big body around the side of the desk, all the while seemingly greatly torn. His expression was full of confusion. Destry watched him anxiously.

"Do those words mean anything to you?" she asked again.

He looked at her. Then, he plopped his buttocks on the edge of his desk and reached out, taking her hands. Flesh against flesh met, the heat from his enormous hands searing her skin. He ended pulling her off the chair, holding her hands against his broad chest as he looked at her with the most confused expression Destry had ever seen.

"You'd better start from the beginning, sweetheart," he said with a mixture of confusion and patience. "Where did you hear those words?"

She was starting to become frightened. "I told you," she repeated. "Those ghosts said them to me. But… but I didn't tell you all of it."

"Then tell me all of it."

She hung her head miserably. "Oh, God," she whispered. "You're going to think I'm crazy."

He squeezed her hands, still clutched against his enormous chest. "No, I'm not. Tell me."

"But I even think I'm crazy," she insisted, her eyes coming up to meet his. "Yesterday when you were talking to your students, I walked around the mound."

"I know. I saw you."

She cocked her head thoughtfully. "I went down to where the passages were," she told him. "I was looking in one of the passages when this wind blew up around me and then I heard someone whisper 'Etain'."

His eyebrows lifted. "Etain?" he repeated. "Is that why you asked me if I'd ever heard the name?"

She nodded. "Yes," she said. "And… and right at sunset, right when the sun's rays hit the stone slabs of the passage where I was standing, something really weird happened."

"What?"

"I'm not lying about this."

"I know. Tell me what happened."

She took a breath for courage, trying to ignore the fact that he was caressing the fingers he was holding so tightly against his muscular chest. "The passage way got really bright," she said, her voice lowering seriously. "And as it brightened, this wind kicked up, like it was blowing out of the tunnel. And I could hear these whispers, like they were coming from inside the mound, like hundreds of people whispering at me. They said 'fanacht, morrigan, gnáthlá agus oiche og ceanna; tar ar cúl do sinne'."

He gazed steadily at her. "The same thing they said to you in your dream."

"Exactly," she looked imploringly at him. "But what does it mean?"

He sighed and continued rubbing her hands, clutched against his chest. He thought a moment. "Well," he said. "The literal translation is *Be still, fair queen, as day and night become the same. Come back to us.*"

She stared at him, digesting his words, and her eyes suddenly widened. "You… you understood that?"

"I did," he replied. "It's an old dialect of Celtic."

She swallowed hard and pulled away from him, a hand to her head as if to hold in her baffled brain. She stumbled back, confused and frightened, before sitting heavily on a small couch he had against the wall.

"But that's impossible," she finally said, looking up at him. "I don't even know Celtic. I don't know anything about it. How could I dream something like that?"

He stood up from his desk, moving slowly in her direction. "You've been in Ireland for a few days," he said. "Maybe you inadvertently heard something like that. Who knows how the mind works?"

She shook her head, baffled. "But that's a full phrase," she said. "More than that, I swear to you that something from that mound touched me yesterday. I could feel it brush against my hand. And I kept hearing 'Etain'. I didn't even know who that was until you told me. How could I imagine that?"

He drew in a long, thoughtful breath before lowering himself next to her on the couch; she was such a little thing compared to his enormous size and he resisted the urge to put his arm around her to comfort her. She seemed like she needed it and he would have very much liked to. Instead, he rested his elbows on his knees, folding his hands to keep them from reaching out to her.

"Who knows?" he said quietly. "I wish I could tell you but that kind of thing is out of my line of work. I wouldn't get so upset about it; it was probably just a fleeting thing."

She looked at him, as close to him as she had ever been. She could see the smoothness of his pale skin and his long white eyelashes.

"So you don't think I'm crazy?" she asked softly.

He smiled faintly. "No," he said. "I think you've got some jet lag and an exhausted mind playing tricks on you."

"I hope so."

"I think I might be able to help, though."

"How?"

"Dinner and drinks. I'd like to show you a little of Dublin and take your mind off your troubles."

A small but genuine smile spread over her lips. "I'm not a charity case, Doctor. You don't need to take me on a pity date because deep down, you really think I'm crazy."

He laughed, displaying his big white teeth and slightly prominent canines. He had a magnificent smile.

"Are you joking?" he snorted. "If anything, people will think you're doing me a favor simply by going out with me. In case you haven't realized it, you're an incredibly beautiful woman. I realize that you're way out of my league, but I'd be honored if you would at least consider the dinner and drinks."

Destry was appalled to realize that she was actually considering it. But there was a larger part of her that was bent on self-protection given what she had just gone through. It was enough to make her greatly indecisive.

"I'd like to," she said honestly. "But... well, it's just not a good idea for me right now. But thank you for the offer."

Based on what her friend Aisling had told him yesterday, he had a pretty good idea why she was rejecting him and he wasn't the least bit offended. Nor was he deterred.

"I'm really a cad, you know," he said softly.

"Why?"

He wriggled his red eyebrows. "Because I'm going to stalk you until you agree to go out with me." As she started to laugh, he grew more animated; he started throwing his big arms around for emphasis. "I'm going to hang out in your hotel lobby and plead my case every time you come out of your room. I may even latch on to your leg and refuse to let go. And if you don't go out with me, I'll... I'll throw myself from the roof and then you'll be sorry."

She shook her head, still snorting with laughter. "Don't do that," she told him. "I'm not worth it."

His blue eyes glimmered with humor, with warmth. "Yes, you are," he insisted, his voice softening. "I know this is supposed to be your honeymoon. I may not be your groom, but I'd certainly like to treat you like a very special lady once or twice while you're here. Please don't turn me down."

Destry stared at him, her smile fading. "Did Aisling tell you that?"

He nodded. "When you walked away from me so quickly yesterday, I thought I had offended you. I told Aisling to apologize to you on my behalf but she said that I hadn't done anything wrong. She told me that you were supposed to be in Dublin on your honeymoon but that it hadn't worked out. So I apologize if I upset you yesterday commenting about the Davenport's grand honeymoon suite."

Destry averted her gaze, away from his handsome face and probing eyes. After a moment, she sighed faintly. "You didn't," she said. "I guess I'm just going to have to get used to the idea."

"What happened?"

She looked at him, sharply, preparing to tell him it was none of his business but she could see that he wasn't trying to invade her privacy. His gentle question felt caring and sincere. She found herself answering him before she really thought about it.

"I was stupid, I guess," she shrugged her shoulders. "We had been dating about a year. He was a professional athlete and I'd heard rumors of him having other women, but I guess I just didn't want to believe it. I thought I could be everything to him. We had this big wedding planned and on the day of the wedding, I'm all dressed up at the church and his best man came in with a note. The note said that he was sorry but he just couldn't go through with the wedding. So I put away my wedding dress and brought Aisling along with me on what was supposed to be my honeymoon. And here I am."

Conor gazed at her, shaking his head with great regret when their eyes met. "Can I say something, please?" he asked softly.

"Sure."

"He is the stupidest man who has ever walked this earth. What fool would turn down a chance to spend the rest of his life with you?"

"You don't really know me; for all you know, I could be a major pain in the ass."

He laughed softly. "If you were, I would have already seen the signs by now."

"The nightmares aren't enough of a sign?"

He shrugged. "Maybe a sign that you're a future mental patient, but not a sign that you're a pain in the arse. Your fiancé is a moron and you're better off without him."

She smiled faintly; somehow, in telling him, it had eased her damaged heart a little. His words made her feel comforted, supported. She shrugged again, looking at her hands.

"I guess I would rather have him back out before the wedding than after," she said. "The main thing is that I'm going to enjoy this trip if it kills me. But this thing with the nightmares is really getting to me. I'm afraid to go back to the hotel and try to sleep even though I'm exhausted."

His gaze drifted over her face. "You look exhausted," he agreed. Then he suddenly looked around, grabbing a pillow from behind him. He wedged it against the arm of the couch where Destry was sitting. "You can lay down here. I've got some work to do at my desk and I'll sit with you for a while. If the nightmares come back, I'll chase them away."

She smiled gratefully. "You really don't have to do that," she insisted. "I've already taken enough of your time."

He waved her off and began shoving her sideways so she would lie down on the couch. "Don't fight with me," he said. "Just lie down. I'll be at my desk if you need me."

"But I can't."

"Why not?"

"Because... well, because we just met each other. This is really strange."

"If you won't go out with me, then at least lie on my couch. It's the least you can do since you're going to break my heart."

She snorted. But the thought of trying to sleep with his enormous, protective presence just a few feet away admittedly brought her comfort. She could feel herself relenting as she lifted an eyebrow at him.

"Well...," she said reluctantly. "You're not going to try anything funny, are you?"

His brow furrowed. "Like what? Whisper old Irish phrases in your ear while you're sleeping?"

"You'd better not."

He grinned. "I won't, I promise."

They smiled at each other for a few moments, the first true genuinely warm moment they had ever shared. He was breaking Destry down with his chivalry and kindness, something she very much needed. She finally lowered herself down onto the couch as he stood up, taking her legs and putting them up on the couch.   He stood over her a moment, watching her get comfortable.

"Are you cozy now?"' he asked.

She snuggled down against the pillow, instantly feeling very sleepy. "Fine," she said. "Thanks, Dr. Daderga. I really appreciate your kindness."

He watched her, realizing he'd probably give everything he owned at the moment for the chance to lie down next to her. He couldn't explain the strong attraction to her or the fact that he wanted to take her into his arms and never let her go. He'd known a lot of attractive women in his life but he'd never known a pull as strong as this one. It was unsettling but marvelous.

"Please call me Conor," he said softly. "And it's my pleasure."

Destry smiled at him as he winked at her and turned back for his desk. She didn't even remember him sitting down behind it before she was fast asleep.

Destry was screaming again before she realized it.

CHAPTER FOUR

Destry was gasping with panic, black terror from the darkness of sleep that was squeezing the breath out of her. Along with the gasping came the tears and it took her a full minute to realize she was wrapped up tightly in someone's arms. Her face was pressed into a warm, broad chest and a deep, soothing voice was speaking softly to her. She could smell fabric softener and deodorant.

"It's all right," Conor was sitting on the couch with Destry smothered in his big, warm embrace. A big hand held her head against his chest, fingers in her hair. "Quiet, now; you're all right. Everything is all right."

Destry's panicked gasps gave way to hysterical weeping and she began to cry as if her heart was broken. He rocked her gently.

"They… they…," she sobbed. "They came back."

His cheek was against the top of her head. "I know," he murmured, his big hand caressing her head. "I heard."

His voice was so sweet, so soothing. Destry forgot about her heartbreak, her sorrows, and allowed herself to feel his comfort. She pressed against him, disoriented, exhausted and half-asleep, as he gently rocked her. It was heavenly. Eventually, her sobs lessened and she shifted so that her right cheek was against his chest. She could hear his heart beating strongly and steadily, finding more comfort than she had ever known in the arms of a stranger. Before she realized it, she was asleep again.

Her next awareness was of Conor speaking softly into the top of her head. He was telling her to wake up and Destry did, gradually, feeling groggy and exhausted. Becoming more oriented, she realized that she was lying against Conor's chest as he sat back against the couch. His big hand was on her head, caressing it, as his soft voice gently brought her around.

"Destry?" he murmured. "Are you awake?"

She sighed heavily, not wanting to move. He was warm and comfortable. "Yes," she whispered.

She swore she felt him kiss the top of her head before speaking. "I'm truly sorry to have to wake you, but I have a class in a few minutes."

"That's okay," she sighed again, forcing herself to wake up. "Oh, my God… that was insane."

His mouth was against the top of her head. "What was?"

His hot breath sent shivers down her spine. "The dreams," she finally lifted her head, looking up at him. He was so close that she could have licked him had she stuck out her tongue. "Why in the hell would they come back again? Have you ever heard of recurring dreams like that?"

He shook his head, realizing he wanted nothing more at that moment than to kiss her. It was a badly misplaced impulse that he struggled against. But to have her in his arms wiped out the memory of every other woman he had ever known; no one had ever been so sweet or soft or warm. No one had ever come close.

He had been sitting at his desk when she had first started to whimper in her sleep. By the time he looked up to see what the trouble was, she had been in full blown hysteria. The only thing he could think to do was to throw his arms around her and hold her tightly, hoping that would give her enough comfort to chase the nightmares away. It had worked, at least for the half-hour he had sat with her in his arms. It had been the best half-hour of his life.

 "No," he said honestly. "But like I said, this is out of my scope of practice. Did they repeat that phrase again?"

She shook her head, exhausted, and collapsed back against him. Conor gladly wrapped her up in his enormous arms.

"It wasn't the same one," she huddled against his broad chest as he held her. "They said... I think they said something like *Tagtha go sinne, morrigan. Naofa... naofa doras uair an grian codail.* Do you know what it means?"

She felt him sigh heavily, thoughtfully, before speaking. "Come to us, fair queen, to the holy door when the sun sleeps."

Destry stopped sniffling. In fact, she froze for a brief moment before her head lifted again, focusing on him. "Really?"

"Really."

"What in the hell does that mean?"

He gazed at her, reaching up to push a stray strand of hair out of her eyes. "I have no idea," he murmured, his eyes inspecting every inch of her lovely face. "But for your dreams to say something different every time... that's pretty strange."

Destry almost forgot about the dream as she stared at him; she could feel the pull between them, something lusty and magnetic, something that frightened and enticed her at the same time. There was something overwhelming about the man, growing stronger by the moment.

"I know," she replied softly, knowing she should probably put some distance between them but unwilling to move. "I've been trying to tell myself since yesterday that all of this is in my mind, but I'm starting to think that it's not. Maybe someone is trying to tell me something."

He lifted a red eyebrow. "Like what?"

She sighed. "I wish I knew," she said. "You're the expert in Irish myths and legends. What do you think?"

He lifted a thoughtful eyebrow as she stared up at him, as if he held all the answers. After a moment, he simply pulled her back against his chest and rested his chin on the top of her head.

"Well," he said, thinking. "The first phrase they spoke to you was *fanacht, morrigan, gnáthlá agus oiche og ceanna; tar ar cúl do sinne'*."

"Say it again."

"*Fanacht, morrigan, gnáthlá agus oiche og ceanna; tar ar cúl do sinne'*."

"Again."

He grinned. "Why?"

"Because I like hearing you say it."

He laughed softly. "'Be still, fair queen, as day and night become the same. Come back to us'," he recited, then continued. "Then the next one was 'Come to us, fair queen, to the holy door when the sun sleeps'."

"What does it all mean?" she asked.

He thought a moment; in spite of the fact that Conor had a doctorate in Celtic and Irish History, plus a second doctorate in Anthropology, he was a man of reason. He was a great teller of stories, myths and legends, but in spite of that, he didn't believe in ghosts or spirits or prophetic dreams. He had to believe there was a rational explanation for such things.

"Do you honestly want to know?" he replied.

"Of course."

He sighed faintly. "I think that you're in a new place, seeing new things, and that you're exhausted and emotional from what happened to you. I think that you're having nutty dreams because your senses have been weakened by everything going on around you. And I further think that somewhere, somehow, you either read or heard those phrases and your subconscious is playing tricks on your tired mind."

Destry suddenly sat up, looking at him with some disappointment and anger. "You think I made this all up?"

"No," he said firmly. "I think your subconscious did."

As he feared, she pulled out of his arms and stood up, unsteadily, her expression exhausted and accusing.

"So you really do think I'm crazy," she spat, jabbing a finger at him. "Look, Dr. Daderga, I told you I wasn't crazy. I told you I really heard this stuff and right now, I really dreamed it. I'm not making it up."

He stood up, holding his hands up to soothe her. "I believe that you didn't make it up," he insisted. "But you asked me what I think and I'm telling you. I think you must have heard these phases some time in your life, maybe so long ago that you don't even consciously remember it, and now they're coming back to you in dreams."

She stared up at him, just looking hurt at this point. After a moment, she simply lowered her gaze and reached down to collect her purse.

"I am really sorry to have bothered you," she said, putting her purse on her shoulder. "Thanks for... well, not calling me crazy in the beginning. At least you waited a little while."

He moved so that he was standing between her and the door. "Please don't leave," he implored softly. "I didn't call you crazy. And I didn't mean to upset you; I really didn't."

She waved him off but she couldn't help but notice he was creating a very big barrier between her and the exit. "You didn't upset me," she said. "But I know I didn't imagine being touched out there at Dowth. I know something touched my hand."

He gazed at her a moment. "You said it was very windy," he reminded her quietly. "It could have been the wind."

She lifted an eyebrow. "You don't think I know the difference between a wind gust and a touch?" She went to him and grabbed one of his gigantic hands, holding it up in her warm fingers. "This is a touch, Dr. Daderga. I know what this feels like. What I felt yesterday felt just like this, only there wasn't anyone there."

He could only concede that he understood what she was saying. Whether or not he believed it was another matter.

"I don't have any explanation for that," he said, holding her hand even as she let his go. "Look; I have a class in a few minutes. Why don't you go back to the hotel and try to get some sleep. I'll ring you around noon to see how you are. If the dreams won't go away, then maybe we need to figure something else out."

She smiled weakly, pulling her hand from his grip when he wouldn't let her go. "I appreciate your offer," she said, "but this isn't your problem. I just wanted to know if you could figure out what those phrases meant. Whatever is going on with me, I'll figure it out."

He regarded her carefully. "You really aren't going to let me take you out, are you?"

She could read the disappointment in his face. In fact, she was starting to feel some disappointment, too, at never seeing the man again. He had been a spot of brightness and comfort in her darkened world.

With a heavy sigh, she moved to him, stood on her tip-toes, and put her soft hand around his thick neck. Pulling his face down to her level, she kissed him gently on the right cheek and quickly stepped back.

"You've been really sweet and incredibly accommodating," she said quietly. "You don't know how much it means to me. Right now, I'm going to take your advice and go back to the hotel and see if I can sleep a little. This whole thing has me kind of rattled."

The kiss to his cheek left Conor with a pounding heart. Had she not moved away from him so quickly, he would have taken her in his arms and kissed her with something more than just a gentle peck. That was kid's stuff. He wanted to kiss her like a man kisses a woman, deeply and passionately, so much so that his hands were beginning to sweat. He wanted to grab her in the worst way.

"You didn't answer my question," he murmured.

"That's because I don't really have an answer for you."

"So there's hope?"

"Maybe." She sighed again, slapping a hand against her thigh in a helpless gesture. "Probably."

His grin returned, as did his complete and utter joy. "Tonight?"

She laughed at his enthusiasm. "Hold on," she said. "I don't know about tonight. Let me sleep a little and recover and we'll go from there."

"That's fair. But I'm still going to ring the hotel later on to see how you are."

Her smile was genuine. "I'd appreciate that."

Since he knew there was hope in him seeing her again on a social, and perhaps romantic level, he stopped blocking the path to the door and escorted her out of his office.

"Is there anything else you want to see that hasn't been included on any of your tours?" he said hopefully. "I'd be happy to be your personal tour guide this weekend."

She laughed softly. "It's not just me; it's Aisling, too."

"She can tag along."

Destry grinned at him. "That's very generous," she sobered as they came to the door that led from his offices out into the main corridor beyond. She paused, gazing up into his pale, handsome face. "Seriously, you've been extremely generous and kind. I can't thank you enough."

He dipped his head graciously. "The pleasure has been all mine, Destry Kenna Caldbeck." He cocked his head. "How'd you get that name, anyway?"

She lifted her eyebrows. "My dad's an old movie buff. I was named after the James Stewart movie of the same name." When he grinned, she shrugged lamely. "Hey; it could have been worse. My younger sister's name is Angel after the John Wayne movie 'Angel and the Badman'. Mom threw in the good Irish names; Angel's middle name is Caitlin. That's what she goes by."

He snorted. "I'm the last one to laugh at names," he said. "My birth name isn't Conor Daderga. It's Conor Peter O'Farrelly. I legally changed it when I got into college and became obsessed with Celtic mythology. I've always felt so misplaced, as if I was born in the wrong time, as if I belonged back in the days when Cuculainn roamed the earth. I wanted to pattern myself after the Irish high warriors so I adopted a true Irish name."

"And O'Farrelly isn't?"

He shrugged. "It is, but there's an old Irish tale called Togail Bruidne Dá Derga, or the Destruction of Da Derga's Hostel, a tale I might add that involves the lovely Etain. I changed my name after reading that tragedy; even as I read the words, it was as if I could picture myself right in the middle of the story. It changed my life and focused me on the true value and richness of my Irish heritage."

He was very passionate in his speech, an animated man with a gift for storytelling. She appreciated that quality, something rarely seen where she came from. Conor was a true anomaly in the world, something she was increasingly coming to appreciate.

"You're the most authentic Irishman I've ever met, that's for sure," she said with a twinkle in her eye, extending her hand to him. "Thanks again for everything."

He took her hand, dwarfing it, his eyes never leaving her beautiful face. "Slán, sweetheart."

She cocked her head. "What does that mean?"

"Farewell. At least until I ring you later on."

She smiled, almost shyly. "Thanks again."

He should have let her go; he really should have. But he couldn't; impulsively, he grasped her face with his enormous hands and slanted his lips hungrily over hers. He could feel her pulling away out of shock, but very quickly, she stopped pulling. The harder he kissed her, the less her resistance. He could feel her caving against him, her soft body melding to his. Conor's hands left her face as his enormous arms wrapped around her body, pulling her tightly against him. What was meant to be a short, sweet kiss turned into something heated and sexual very quickly, broken up by the sounds of students entering in the corridor for morning classes.

Before they realized it, they were standing about three feet apart. Conor had no idea how they got so far apart; last thing he remembered, he was tasting her sweet musky flavor with a hint of cherry lip gloss and loving it. Now they were standing a few feet apart and staring at each other as students began to walk by, filling the old corridor as classes prepared to commence. Conor looked at her apprehensively.

"Should I apologize for that?" he whispered.

Destry stared at him a moment, nodding, then shaking her head. She threw up her hands. "I have no idea," she hissed.

"I don't want to apologize for something that good."

Destry licked her lips, tasting him on her flesh, unbalanced by the entire circumstance. She averted her gaze as she began to walk away.

"Have a good day, Dr. Daderga," she said as she passed him.

He reached out and grasped her arm, forcing her to stop. She wouldn't look at him as he spoke. "I probably shouldn't have done that but I'm not sorry I did, if that makes any sense. I don't want to make you uncomfortable."

"You didn't."

From her stiff stance, he wasn't buying it. "I... I don't know what came over me," he insisted softly. "It's just that you're so... and I'm so attracted to you that... Destry, I'm sorry. I'm truly sorry if I offended or upset you. I swear to God I'm not trying to get you into bed. I just wanted to kiss you. I've never wanted to do anything so badly in my life."

She did look at him, then, forcing a weak smile. "Don't worry about it," she patted the hand on his arm and he reluctantly let her go. "I'll talk to you later."

"Really?"

"Really."

She took a few steps away before coming to a halt, turning to see if he was still standing there. He was, looking at her, anxious and distressed. Destry could feel herself easing.

"If it makes any difference, I liked it, too."

With that, she turned and continued down the hall, very quickly. Conor stood there, watching her perfect butt in her tight jeans and the sexy slope of her torso. He could have watched that woman's butt for the rest of his life. But she eventually disappeared from view and he went back into his office, struggling to compose himself before his class. Try as he might, he just couldn't shake her. It made for an interesting class when his students couldn't figure out why the normally unflappable Dr. Daderga seemed so scatterbrained.

Promptly at noon, he rang the hotel only to find out that she had gone missing.

CHAPTER FIVE

"I went on that tour this morning of religious sites around Dublin," Aisling said. "She was supposed to come with me but she said she wasn't feeling well. And you said that she came to see you this morning?"

Conor and Aisling were in Conor's ten-year-old Vauxhall wagon that had seen better days, tearing north on the M1 motorway from Dublin to Drogheda in the midst of a pouring rainstorm. They were nearly to Drogheda and then Dowth was another few miles to the east of the city.

"She did," Conor held tight to the steering wheel as the rain pounded. "Like I told you earlier, she told me that spirits or ghosts talked to her when she was out here yesterday and she had bad dreams about it all night. She came to see me because these ghosts, or whatever they were, were speaking to her in a language she didn't understand. She thought I might. She was upset about it and something tells me that she might have come back out here again."

Aisling watched the weather ominously. "But why?"

He shook his head, frustrated and concerned. "She seemed to think her nightmares centered around Dowth because that's where everything started. Since you have no idea where she is, and she doesn't know the city very well, I just have this odd feeling that she's come back out here to figure out why she seems to be having these nightmares."

"But what if she's been kidnapped? Don't you think we should call the cops?"

"If she's not at Dowth, then we will."

Aisling looked at him, feeling rather guilty about the whole thing. "I know she didn't sleep last night because I woke up in the middle of the night and could see the bathroom light on. When I got up and knocked on the door, she said she was reading in the bathroom because she couldn't sleep and didn't want to wake me up. Then, this morning, she said she didn't feel well so I went on the tour without her." She shook her head with regret. "I shouldn't have left her. I should have stayed with her."

Conor could see their exit coming up, the roundabout to the N51 highway east. His sense of urgency was so great that he was flooring the car when he thought he could get away with it.

"You couldn't have known," he replied, though he was feeling some guilt as well. "Maybe I'm the one to blame for this. When she came to see me this morning, she repeated the phrases she had heard in her dreams. I could see how upset she was about it. Maybe...maybe I just should have stayed with her until she calmed down."

Aisling shook her head again, gazing out at the driving rain. "Why?" she said. "She's not your responsibility. But you were able to make sense out of those phrases from her dreams?"

He nodded. "Indeed I was," he replied. "They were a form of Old Gaelic. I told her that somewhere, somehow, she must have heard the phrases and tucked them back into her subconscious. She thought that ghosts were talking to her and I told her that there had to be a rational explanation."

Aisling just shook her head, baffled by the entire event. "I can't believe she didn't say anything to me about it," she said. "I've known her since we were ten years old and she tells me absolutely everything."

Conor thought about the implications of that; his growing interest and concern in Destry prompted him to ask questions he hoped Aisling didn't consider probing. He tried to be cool about it.

"Has she ever pulled anything like this before?" he asked.

Aisling shook her head. "No way," she said firmly. "Not Des. It's not like her to leave and not tell anyone. She's one of the most normal, down-to-earth people I know. She's, like, the most perfect person you'll ever meet. She doesn't smoke or drink, she even flosses her teeth every night. Did she tell you that she's a nurse?"

"She did."

Aisling pointed a finger at him. "She's not just any nurse; she volunteers her skills to Doctors without Borders and she's gone to Haiti twice to give free medical care to refugees. She's like a modern-day Florence Nightingale." She suddenly shook her head again, looking out of the window as the rain pounded. "What that jerk did to her on her wedding day... I swear, so many people want to kill him. Her dad probably put a contract out on him already."

Conor was forced to slow down in order to take the roundabout. "How did she meet him?"

Aisling held on to the door handle as they took the circular turn. "He's a wide receiver for the San Diego Chargers," she said, looking at him. "Do you know who they are?"

For the first time since getting into the car, he grinned. "Yes, I know who they are," he said, changing lanes as they entered the N51 motorway. "I'm a fan of American Football."

"Oh," Aisling continued with her story, gazing out over the new highway. "Anyway, he was a wide receiver and she was one of the Charger Girls, their cheerleading squad. She only tried out for the squad because some of her friends dared her to but she ended up making it. Boy, was she hot in that little Charger outfit. She got a boob job and she looked like... uh, that was probably too much information, right?"

Conor fought off a broader grin. "Not at all. It explains why I... well, that *would* be too much information, so forget it."

Aisling snorted. "Well, she was the hottest cheerleader they had, at any rate. She was even on the cover of their calendar last year. She was smoking."

"She still is," he cast her a long look before refocusing on the road, causing Aisling to giggle.

"I saw that you noticed," she teased him. He just wriggled his eyebrows and she continued. "Anyway, I guess he saw her on the sidelines and found out who she was. The cheer squad isn't supposed to fraternize with the players, but he really pursued her heavily. He was a nice guy in the beginning but really full of himself. It was clear that he put himself before her, in almost everything. I got to the point where I just kind of tolerated him because she was so in love with him, but when he left her at the altar... well, that went beyond even what I thought he was capable of. What an ass."

Conor didn't say anything as he read the motorway signs that were coming into view. "Is she into professional athletes, then?"

Aisling gazed out of the window at the wet, green countryside. "Not really," she said. "She's dated cops, firemen, salesmen... she even dated an actor once. But she always says it doesn't matter what he is but who he is on the inside. She seemed to attract all of the superficial guys because of her looks, hardly any that were nice to her just because she was sweet and genuine. But after this debacle, I'm sure she's sworn men off forever."

Conor changed lanes again as their exit approached. "That would be a real tragedy."

Aisling grinned, turning to look at him. "I don't think she's dated a college professor before. Do you want me to put a good word in for you, Dr. Daderga?"

He grinned but wouldn't look at her. "To a woman like that? Only in my dreams."

"Oh, I don't know," Aisling's brown eyes twinkled. "She seemed to enjoy the conversation with you yesterday. I think she kind of liked you."

He looked at her, hardly daring to hope. "Do you really think so?"

Grinning, Aisling pointed at the highway sign coming up. "There's our exit."

Conor refocused on the road, taking the off ramp and taking a left onto Littlegrange Road. The rain was coming down in sheets as they headed south, the road eventually turning into Dowth Road as they neared the mound. They could see it in the distance, a great green loaf rising above the flat countryside, and he sped up. When they finally pulled into the carpark, water and mud sprayed as he came to an abrupt halt. He threw the car into Park and turned to Aisling.

"You stay here," he told her. "If she doesn't want to be found, she might run from me. I need you to stay here in case she runs; you can see the entire mound from here. If she takes off and you see her, I want you to honk the horn like crazy. All right?"

Aisling nodded, watching him get out of the car. "Do you want an umbrella?"

He shook his head, pulling his crumpled Drogheda United baseball-style hat out of the backseat and pulling onto his spiked hair. Slamming the car door, he zipped up his rain coat and began to walk around the base of the mound, heading towards the southern tunnels.

The rain was letting up somewhat as he made his way around the east side of the mound. It was heavy with wet foliage and protected him from the light rain that was now falling. The clouds above were even starting to clear and patches of blue appeared. Moving through the dripping brush, he came upon the first of the three tunnels. Pulling out his torch, he flashed it down into the tunnel but saw nothing; it was dark and cold.

He moved on to the second tunnel and shined his torch in that one, but it was black and empty. The third tunnel was several feet away and he went to hit, pulling out his torch and preparing to shine it into that tunnel. But as he took a step into the dark archway, he immediately spied a lump on the ground just a few feet from the door.

Startled, he flashed his torch downward and saw Destry sitting with her back against the wall, huddled in a ball. Her knees were up, her arms embracing them and her face was buried in the tops of her knees. When the flashlight fell on her, she yelped in fright, her head swiftly coming up. Conor jumped, too, because she had. He snapped off the torch so it wouldn't blind her.

"Destry?" he went into a crouch in the small tunnel, moving towards her in the wet earth. "What are you doing here, sweetheart? You scared Aisling to death when she couldn't find you."

Destry looked at him; she was pale, her beautiful face streaked where she had wept and wiped her face with dirty hands. She was also wet, shivering in the darkness.

"How did you find me?" she asked.

He could see how cold she was and he knelt beside her, taking her hands into his warm palms and feeling that they were like ice. "I took a wild guess when Aisling said you were missing," he told her. "How did you get here?"

His warm hands felt so good. She looked down at his massive mitts as they closed around her small ones and fat tears began to roll down her cheeks.

"I took a taxi," she whispered. "It cost me a fortune."

He caressed her cold hands, trying to rub some warmth back into her fingers. "Why did you do it?"

She wiped at her cheeks. "I tried to go back to sleep this morning when I went back to the hotel," she wept softly. "Every time I closed my eyes, those whispers came back. And there were faces; white faces, scary faces. I couldn't really see them clearly but they were there, trying to talk to me. Then I'd wake up scared, fall back asleep again, and then wake up screaming all over again. It happened four times. I know you told me that it was my subconscious mind playing tricks on me, but I just don't think it is. Nothing like this has ever happened to me before."

He could see how upset she was and he put a big hand on her head. "Oh, sweetheart," he murmured. "I'm so sorry. But it still doesn't explain why you came back here."

"Because," she sounded angry. "I figured if I couldn't get away from the whispers, then I'd at least try to make friends with them. Maybe they'll leave me alone then. So I came out here and I've been talking to them all afternoon."

"Have they talked back?"

She looked at him reluctantly. "No," she said, glancing around the dark tunnel and sighing heavily. "It's been quiet and still, just like this. Oh, hell; maybe I am crazy. I just don't know anymore."

She hung her head again and started to cry. He sat down beside her and opened up his jacket, putting it around her as he pulled her against his big, warm torso. She was freezing cold and he held her close, trying to warm her.   She wept softly and he hugged her, his cheek against the top of her head.

"Don't cry," he murmured. "I'm sure whatever this is, it will pass. If it doesn't, I'll volunteer to spend the nights with you and chase the bad dreams away. They wouldn't dare tangle with me."

Her face was against his chest, a warm and comforting thing. After a moment, she lifted her head and he looked down at her, realizing she was smiling. The wet, bright blue eyes gazed up at him.

"You *are* pretty scary," she agreed. "You're a pretty big guy."

He lifted a red eyebrow at her. "Big and skilled in the art of warfare from the time of the Romans up until the end of the medieval period. I can fight with clubs, swords, fists, feet, spears, knives and anything else that can even remotely be used as a weapon. If those ghosts know what's good for them, they'll leave you the hell alone."

Her tears were forgotten at his chivalrous declaration. "You can really fight like that?"

He nodded firmly. "I teach a Medieval Warfare class. I get my students out in the cricket field to the north of the campus and we learn the art of real war, not this sissy sophisticated stuff that we do nowadays. Back in the day, men fought hand to hand and only the strongest survived."

She smiled faintly. "I saw all of the weapons you had on the wall of your office."

"I'm very proud of my collection."

"Ever use them on anybody?"

He wriggled his eyebrows. "Not yet. But if the university is attacked by barbarian hordes, I'm ready."

She was feeling better with him around; his warmth, his comforting presence. She had spent the past several hours sitting in the tunnel, watching it rain outside and inviting the ghosts to talk to her again.

Once he put his big arms around her and his warmth began to envelope her, she began to realize how exhausted she really was and how foolish it had been to come all the way out here just because of some bad dreams. Maybe she really *was* losing her mind. A botched wedding, grief and exhaustion could do strange things to even the strongest person. She sighed again and looked around.

"Well," she said after a moment. "Now that you're here, I really feel like an idiot for coming out here. You didn't have to come after me."

He waggled his red eyebrows at her dramatically. "Yes, I did."

She chuckled softly. "I was just sure that... oh, I don't know; I guess I was just sure that I would experience something again."

He leaned down and whispered hotly in her ear, his lips against her flesh. "In am, sárálainn bean."

She turned to look at him, feeling more than the heat from his body; she was feeling the heat from his gaze and from his words. She found herself watching his full, soft lips, remembering how they tasted.

"What does that mean?" she asked breathlessly.

He smiled faintly. "It means 'You will in time, beautiful girl'."

"Will what?"

"Experience something again. Maybe better than before."

She met his smile, feeling giddy and tremulous against him. He had that effect on her. But her self-defense was kicking in, the last shred of protection between her broken heart and the outside world. She looked away from him but there was a smile on her lips.

"You're sweet, Dr. Daderga," she said. "And I'm wet and freezing. I assume you brought a car so I don't have to take out a loan to pay for a taxi back to Dublin?"

He nodded. "Aisling is waiting for us in my car. We should probably head back before she comes looking for us."

Destry nodded, somewhat reluctantly, looking around the tunnel one last time as if hoping the ghosts would come forth, just once, so she could prove to Conor that she wasn't insane. As nice as he was, she knew that he must have some doubt. As she turned to him, she caught a glimpse of the clouds clearing outside the mound. The sun was sitting low on the horizon, creating brilliant orange and yellow rays that warmed the wet countryside. She nodded her head in the direction of the setting sun.

"Look," she said. "Another beautiful Irish sunset."

He turned to look at the setting sun even though his attention was on the feeling of her in his arms. As he watched the sun set, he realized that he didn't want this time with her to end, this magic that he was feeling every time he looked at her. It was an odd sensation, something between adoration and excitement. From the moment he saw her, he had experienced sensations that he had never experienced before, with anyone. As the sunset deepened, he pulled her more tightly against him, watching the dying rays.

"I'm glad I found you out here today," he said quietly.

She looked at him, his strong profile warmed by the orange rays. "What do you mean?"

He turned to look at her, very close to her face. "Other than the relief that you are in one piece, I'm glad I got to share the sunset with you."

She looked at him, his intense blue eyes, and felt as if they had reached some sort of pinnacle. Whatever she was feeling for the man, whatever anticipation or excitement he represented, the truth was that she wasn't emotionally strong enough for it at the moment. It was time for some honesty.

"And I'm glad I got to share it with you, too," she said softly. "But... I'm not sure this can go any further."

"What can't go any further?"

She lifted her eyebrows. "I know it's presumptive of me to anticipate what you may or may not be thinking, but you and me... I mean, not that there is a you and me, but...."

He cut her off. "I wish there was. I'd give my right arm for it."

She grew serious. "Aisling told you why I'm here, right?"

"She did."

"Then you know the last thing on my mind is a hook-up. I can't; I'm not emotionally ready for anything close to that."

He knew that. But he wasn't going to give up hope. "I'm a patient man," he told her. "When you're ready, I'll be here."

Her brow furrowed. "Are you crazy? I live in California."

"It's only a plane ride away."

She shook her head at him as he tried to make the situation seem simpler than it was. "It's six thousand miles away."

He shifted his big body, his enormous arms tightening around her. Destry felt his heat, his power, and it began to weaken her resolve. His handsome face loomed in front of her, half of it illuminated by the sunset.

"I'm going to try to explain this, so listen closely," he said, his tone a gentle growl. "When I saw you yesterday, no one I had ever seen in my life caught my eye like you did. Here I was, teaching a class, and an angel walked right into my midst. I don't know how else to describe it. Then, when you came to my office today, it was like my prayers had been answered and there you were again. And the kiss… Destry, I don't know if I can ever kiss another woman again because you've ruined them all for me. No other kiss will ever come close. If I died tomorrow, I would die a happy man. So a six thousand mile plane ride doesn't concern me; I'd go to the Arctic if that's where you were. Anywhere you are, I'll follow."

She gazed at him with an expression something between disbelief and pleasure. "Nobody talks like that, Conor."

"Like what?"

"Like something out of a romance novel. You sound like Prince Charming."

He grinned. "I hope so," he said, his blue eyes glittering. "Is it working?"

She laughed softly. "I don't know. Maybe."

"I'm willing to live the rest of my life on a maybe."

She was incredulous. "Just for me?"

His smile faded as his gaze grew intense. "Only for you."

Destry wasn't sure what more she could say; she had stated her case, sort of, and he was making his desires plain. She stared at him, trying to figure out his true motivation; infatuation? Insanity? She wondered.

"But you don't even know me," she said softly, earnestly. "You just met me."

He unwound a big arm from around her torso, taking her chin between his thumb and forefinger. Turning her head slightly, he kissed her gently on the cheek.

"I know enough," he whispered, turning her face again and kissing her nose delicately. "What I don't know, I can learn. What I can't learn, I can feel."

She closed her eyes as his mouth moved to the other cheek, kissing her with great tenderness. "Oh, my God," she breathed. "Are you for real?"

Conor eyes were closed as well. He didn't miss a beat as he swooped in for her lips. "Very real," he murmured as his mouth clamped down over hers.

As Conor and Destry lost themselves in a deeply passionate kiss, the rays from the setting sun were beginning to fall on the entrance of ancient stone. Just as they did yesterday, the soft yellow rays hit the porous slabs, warming them, creating the same odd glow as they had yesterday, only tonight the glow was stronger and more potent. An odd hum was also beginning to churn as the rock heated up, reverberating through the slab with an ancient song.

Had Conor not been so consumed with Destry in his arms, he might have noticed that the sunlight was now streaming in through the tunnel, hitting the back of the chamber as it had done for every Spring and Fall equinox for five thousand years. The old stones were positioned just so, creating the right conditions for worlds to collide at just this place, just this time.

The old mound of Dowth had never been a burial chamber; it had been a chamber where ancient man had moved through time and worlds as easily as moving from one field to the other. But only under the correct conditions, when the days and nights were of the same length, and the stars were aligned just so. This was one of those times. Those caught within the mound would walk between worlds in echoes of ancient dreams.

One moment, Conor had Destry trapped firmly in his arms and in the next, a brilliant flash of light blinded him. It was enough to pull his attention from Destry, who gasped with fright at the blinding white light. But her gasp was the last thing he heard before the white light drowned out everything conscious thought, every waking awareness.

And then... there was darkness.

CHAPTER SIX

There was a soft wind, blowing gently about her. Destry was half-conscious, feeling the breeze about her. Something cold was tickling her face but she wasn't lucid enough to brush it away. She was in a dreamy daze, somewhere between light and dark, and the only sound that met her ears was that of birds singing overhead.

Consciousness came and went. She drifted into darkness again, a sweet and blissful place, until warm hands were on her and she gradually became aware that someone had lifted her up. She felt a gentle touch on her cheeks, stroking her.

"Destry?" she could hear the distinctly male voice. "Can you hear me, sweetheart? Open your eyes. Open them and look at me."

Destry was trying; in fact, she was trying very hard but she just couldn't seem to open her eyes. When she was able to marginally peep them open, the light was so bright that she closed her eyes again. The darkness swarmed around her and she drifted off.

Conor could see that she had passed out again. He was fairly woozy himself but he fought it; looking around, they were in heavy foliage, remarkably dry, as the weak sunlight beat down through the tree canopy overhead. Had he not been feeling so ill or confused it would have been a lovely sight. But all he could manage to feel at the moment was disorientation, confusion and nausea.

His last memory had been of kissing Destry in the dank, cold tunnel of Dowth mound. It had been hot and delicious, everything he could have imagined it would be. Then he had awoken in the overgrown grass, staring straight up at the sky, wondering what in the hell had happened. He felt as if he'd been on the losing end of a fight as he struggled to clear his head, sitting up slowly as the world rocked. He truly had no idea what had happened. Over to his left, he could see Destry crumpled on her side like a rag doll.

Heart in his throat, he forgot about his spinning head as he struggled to Destry's side. Carefully, he rolled her on to her back, very carefully inspecting her pale face to see if he could see any visible damage. At this point, not knowing what had happened, he ran his hands down her arms and legs, feeling for broken bones, but she was intact.   Then he carefully scooped her into his arms and tried to rouse her.

Destry was struggling to come around but she was still fairly out of it. Conor wasn't feeling much better but at least he was upright. He held her against his broad chest, watching her sigh and twitch, before taking a look back up at the mound. He expected to see it exploded outward at the very least, because something had obviously thrown them clear of the mound; they were at least twelve or more feet away from it.

It took him a moment to realize that the mound of Dowth was very much intact and extremely overgrown. In fact, he could barely see the tunnel they had been huddled in for all of the growth around it. His blue eyed gaze drifted over the lines of the mound, something he knew very well, but it just didn't look the same as it had a few minutes earlier. Puzzlement began to sprout.

"What the...?" he muttered.

His brow furrowed in confusion and he began to look around; nothing was as he remembered it; no fences, no farm houses, no neatly tended fields. It was all wild meadow as far as he could see. It was all very weird but he shoved his bewilderment aside. He had no idea what had happened to them other than some kind of natural explosion and decided the best course of action would be to return to his car and get Destry to a hospital. Then maybe he needed to get his head checked, too, because things didn't look the same as they did just a few minutes earlier. Maybe the explosion had given him a concussion or something. He certainly felt like it.

He gently scooped Destry into his arms, cradling her carefully as he made his way around the east side of the mound. Here, too, it looked extremely overgrown and the entrance tunnels on this side were nearly completely blocked off with fallen stone and bramble. Greatly perplexed, he rounded the side of the mound with the expectation of finding the carpark dead ahead. He came to an abrupt halt when he realized there was nothing there but open, green field. Everything was gone.

Conor stared at the area where his car should have been, starting to wonder if he hadn't lost his mind. Nothing was as it should be or where he left it and he was struggling against an increasingly strong sense of dread. As he stood there with Destry cradled in his arms, trying to figure out what he should do next, the bramble off to his left suddenly rattled.

Startled, he whirled around in time to see a very small, willowy woman push through the trees with three small children at her side. His brow furrowed as he realized the woman was wearing a nightgown. Or, at least, he thought it was a nightgown; it was as white as she was, the color blending into her skin, all wispy and flowing. She also had a walking stick in her hand, a stick that was twice her height.

As the trees parted and the woman drew closer, he could see that she was a younger woman, her white hair long and straight, and the children with her weren't as much children as they were midgets or dwarfs. He truly had no idea; they were odd little people with big hands and big heads, and they were dressed in raggedy pajamas as they suddenly rushed at him, squealing. Startled, and at a disadvantage with an unconscious woman in his arms, Conor backed off. The woman in the nightgown lifted a hand to him in greeting.

"*Mo Thiarna*," she said. "*Dia bheannaithe linn ar an lá seo de laethanta le do thuairisceán. Táimid ag guí ar an lá seo.*"

Conor stared at her. It was an extremely archaic form of Irish Gaelic, something very odd and out of place in this modern world. Although he understood her completely, her words had no meaning to him. *My lord, God has blessed us on this day of days with your return. We have prayed for this day.*

"*Dia,*" he replied. "*Duit go bhfuil an bhean bhí gortaithe. An féidir leat glaoch ar chabhair leighis?*"

This woman is injured; can you call for medical assistance? He tried not to sound too panicked or too bewildered as he asked. Getting help for Destry was all he could think about at the moment; everything else, all of the weirdness and disorientation, would have to wait. But the woman smiled faintly at him.

 "You do not remember me, do you?" she said in her heavy Gaelic. "'Tis of no concern, my lord. You will remember in time."

Conor regarded her, shaking his head after a moment and replying in her dialect. "I'm sorry, I don't know who you are. Do you have a mobile phone with you?"

There was no word for 'phone' in Gaelic, so he had to go with the best translation he could. The woman cocked her head, looking rather amused. "I am Padraigan the White," she said. "Your memory will return. But you must come with me now, quickly. They must not find you here."

Conor had no idea what she was talking about. He thought the woman was a little crazy so he started to walk away, thinking it would be best to put distance between them, but she trailed after him.

"Please, my lord," she said with growing insistence. "You must not go that way. You must come with me. You must...!"

He suddenly came to a halt, whirling on her. "Look," he cut her off, the distinct look of agitation on his face. "This lady is injured. She needs a doctor. Can you at least call for a taxi so I can get her to a hospital?"

The little people collected at Conor's feet and began to tug at him, inspecting his jeans. He actually kicked one of them away when the man got too close to his crotch. Padraigan put her stick out and tapped one of the little folk on the shoulder, causing all of them to look at her.

"Quickly," she commanded softly. "Get the horses. We must return them swiftly or all will be lost."

"What are you talking about?" Conor asked, growing more distressed. "Can you even understand what I'm saying? I need to get this woman to a hospital."

For the first time, Padraigan's gaze moved to Destry, lying still and pale in Conor's enormous arms. Her gaze softened as she studied the lovely face and a hand came up as if to touch her, but just as quickly pulled away. There was reverenced in her expression, in her tone, as she spoke.

"Fanacht, morrigan," she whispered. "Gnáthlá agus oiche og ceanna; tar ar cúl do sinne."

Conor's eyes narrowed dangerously and he took a step back as if to protect Destry from this strange and mysterious woman. He was becoming seriously upset by all of this, the strange people, the odd land, and the fact that he didn't feel well at all. Something terrible had happened but it was like living a nightmare; he couldn't seem to get any help. No one understood what he needed. Short of walking to Drogheda, which was just a few miles to the east, he wasn't sure what more he could say or do to stress his urgency. Now, with this bizarre woman repeating the very words that Destry had sworn she had heard in her dreams, he was at his limit of patience.

"Where in the hell did you hear that?" he hissed.

Padraigan looked at him, not at all offended by his tone. The High King had always been extremely protective of his wife, a woman he was deeply and hopelessly in love with. Their love story was legendary, so much so that vying factions in the kingdom had gone to great lengths to preserve it. Now, they were back and the situation threatened to explode all over again. And it would if she could not get the man to safety.

"I called to her and she heard me," she replied simply. "That is why you are here, my lord. She brought you here. You must come with me."

Conor's fury was being overwhelmed by confusion and, if he were to admit it, some fear. "What are you talking about?" he demanded. "Who in the hell are you? And no more of this bullshit you've been feeding me. Who in the hell are you really?"

Sounds of horses could be heard and they both turned to see the little people returning with four horses. But these weren't any horses; they were shaggy and fat, oddly shaped. Padraigan motioned towards the beasts.

"Come, my lord," her calm tone now had a sense of urgency to it. "We must hurry."

Conor stood his ground. "Hurry where?" he demanded. "I'm not going anywhere until you tell me who you are."

Padraigan remained calm. "I told you, my lord," she said. "I am Padraigan the White. I am your *litrithe.* You do not remember now but you will in time. You must trust me and come with me; otherwise, your life is in great danger."

Conor just stared at the woman, the sense of dread that had been gnawing at him now sprouting wings and taking flight. "My sorceress?" he repeated, translating her word. "What is…?"

"There is no time, my lord. You must come now. I will explain everything when we are safe."

Conor pulled Destry tighter, glancing around to the overgrown mound, the heavy foliage, the fields that were wild and untamed. Overhead, clouds skipped across the unnaturally blue sky. It all looked fairly normal to him but something was different, something he couldn't put his finger on. His defiance began to slip in favor of genuine fear.

"What in the hell is going on?" he finally pleaded, a mere whisper compared to his usual tone.

Padraigan sensed his despair; she had known this would be his reaction and struggled to get the man moving without sitting down and telling him the entire story of his existence. She would do it later, when they were safe. But at this moment, they needed to leave. The urgency was growing.

"Please," Padraigan begged. "I will tell you everything once we reach safety. Will you please trust me?"

Conor wasn't sure he had a choice but he really didn't want to go with her. He wanted to find his car, but his car wasn't there and neither was the carpark, or Aisling, or the small farm that sat just to the east of the mound. Nothing was as he remembered it. It began to occur to him that the blast that had thrown him and Destry clear of the mound had done something. He wasn't sure yet, but something had happened.

One way or the other, he had to find help for Destry. With no car and no phone on him, since he had left it in his car, he thought that perhaps he should go with the woman. There was the larger lure of taking Destry someplace safe; once at the woman's house, maybe she had a landline phone he could use. And he reckoned that if he didn't feel comfortable, he could just leave. Drogheda was about a five mile walk to the east. He'd carry Destry all the way to Dublin to find help for her if he had to.

Without another word, he began to walk towards the horses. Padraigan softly commanded her three little friends to produce the fastest horse for Conor, but he looked rather blankly as a shaggy cream-colored horse was produced. There was no saddle, at least not one he had ever seen; it was a series of heavy blankets held together with a frame of wood for the seat of the saddle.

"Oh, God," he grunted to himself. "A horse? I haven't ridden a horse in years."

"Mount your steed, my lord."

He just shook his head, looking at Destry, wondering how he was going to mount the horse and hold her at the same time. After a moment, he sighed heavily. "How in the hell am I going to do this?"

In his arms, Destry suddenly stirred. She threw up a hand, which ended up thumping him on the cheek. He gazed down at her, seeing that her eyes were marginally open. The hand that had smacked him in the cheek went to her head as if to block out a throbbing headache and her eyes closed again.

"Destry?" he said softly. "Can you hear me?"

This time, she responded. "Yes," she whispered, the bright blue eyes slowly opening again. "What's going on?"

He sighed heavily. "I'm not sure yet," he said honestly. "How do you feel?"

She was quiet a moment; so far, she hadn't tried to move anything but her hand and she remained tucked against his chest, her open eyes staring into his shirt. He could feel her great, heavy sigh.

"Like I've been thrown off a building," she stirred again, this time lifting her head and squinting in the light. "What happened?"

His gaze was soft on her. "I don't know," he said quietly. "One minute I was in the tunnel with you and in the next minute, we were both lying on the grass."

She gazed up at him, her bright blue against his sky blue. "Are you okay?"

He smiled faintly. "I'm fine," he said gently. "I'm more worried about you."

She reached up and wound her arms around his neck, pulling herself up so that she was sitting up somewhat. But as she struggled to settle herself, she caught movement out of the corner of her eye. Padraigan came into view, an unfamiliar and somewhat odd sight, and Destry startled with fright.

"Oh, God," she gasped, suddenly pressed up against Conor as close as she could without actually crawling inside the man. "Who's that?"

Conor looked at the small, thin woman with the dirty pale nightgown on. "She says her name is Padraigan," he said quietly. "She says... well, she says a hell of a lot of weird things, but she mostly says we need to get out of here because we're in danger."

Destry's head came up, the bright blue eyes wide with fear and disorientation. "What danger?"

He shook his head, his gaze on the strange woman and her three companions. "I don't know," he murmured. "They won't say but they want us to come with them."

Destry looked over her shoulder at the very small woman with the extremely pale face before turning back to Conor, throwing her arms around his neck and burying her face against his shoulder.

"I just want to go back to the hotel," she muttered. "I need to lie down. Please take me back."

He sighed faintly. "I would, except the car is gone."

Her head came up, her face within inches of his as she fixed him in the eye. "Where did it go?" she suddenly scowled. "Did Aisling take it? Where in the hell did she go? Oh, my God, my head is killing me."

Her head flopped back down on his shoulder and Conor laid his cheek against the top of her head, rocking her gently. In spite of the bizarre and concerning circumstances, he had her just where he wanted her. He could have stayed like this forever. But Padraigan approached the pair timidly, rattling him out of his fantasy world.

"Please, my lord," she said. "We must leave immediately."

Destry's head came up again, her eyes wide as she looked at him. "What did she say?" she hissed. "What kind of language is that?"

Conor pursed his lips reluctantly; he didn't particularly want to tell her, fearful that it might set her off. But he had no choice.

"Gaelic Irish," he said quietly.

Her face screwed up, confused. "Doesn't she speak English?"

Conor looked at the tiny wisp of a woman "Do you understand English?

Padraigan stared at him, having no idea what he had said. After a moment of confusion, she pointed to the horses again.

"Please, my lord," she begged. "Please ride with me to safety. Time grows short and your children await."

Conor's eyebrows lifted. "Children?" he repeated. "What children?"

Padraigan's gaze moved between Conor and Destry as a faint smile graced her lips. "Your sons," she said. "Perhaps they will help you remember."

Destry was looking at Conor as the woman spoke her bizarre language. It was clear that he was communicating with her but Destry couldn't understand a word. She felt like she was on another planet. Her head was killing her and her body ached terribly, and she was feeling woozy and weary. With a big surge of strength, she suddenly pushed herself out of Conor's enormous arms and almost fell to the ground.

Conor steadied her as she gained her feet and her balance but she shrugged him off. Looking around, she spied the mound several yards away and her eyebrows lifted; it was lumpy and overgrown with foliage. It didn't look anything like the well-manicured mound she had arrived at a few hours earlier. It didn't even look like the same relic, in any way. An odd sense of foreboding swept her.

"What happened to the mound?" she asked, pointing.

He turned to look at it. "I have no idea," he said quietly. "It doesn't look like it did just a few minutes ago."

Destry's hand went to her head, a gesture of utter bafflement, as she started to walk in the direction of the mound. "It's all covered with bushes and grass," she said, overwhelmed with confusion and curiosity. She turned to Conor. "You said we were thrown out of the tunnel?"

He was walking after her. "Yes," he replied. "When I woke up, we were about three or four meters from the tunnel entrance."

Destry wasn't feeling at all well but her sense of curiosity, and fear, were taking over. "Then there must have been an explosion," she was trying to be logical about it. "Is it possible that the explosion threw us out and made it look like this? It looks like some of the tunnels are collapsed."

He just shook his head. "I doubt it," he said. "Whatever damage you see looks as if it has been that way for years. And none of the overgrowth has been disturbed, as it would have been by an explosion."

She couldn't wrap her mind around his assertion. "But there has to have been an explosion," she insisted. "How else would we have been blown out of the tunnel?"

Conor was feeling just as much trepidation as she was but he was more in control of it. "I have no idea," he replied. "But it happened."

She looked at him, the bright blue eyes pleading and searching. "But how?" she demanded softly, then her eyes grew suspicious. "Were we gassed? Maybe someone gassed us and then dragged us outside to rob us."

He almost laughed but couldn't quite bring himself to do it; she was serious and so was he. It was a serious situation.

 "We would have seen someone, or heard them," he took a couple of steps and ended up very close to her, looking down into her lovely face. "Even though my attention was on you, I'm sure I would have heard someone sneaking up to gas us."

"Did you check your pockets? Is your wallet still there?"

"I left my wallet in the car."

She pursed her lips as if he had just made an awful mistake. "Now Aisling has it and is probably charging up all of your credit cards."

He grinned. "If she does, I'll take it out on you."

"Oh, yeah? And how are you going to do that?'"

"Do you really want to know?"

"Yes. No. Well, maybe."

Conor laughed softly. They had come to a halt about twenty feet from the mound, facing each other, when an object of some kind suddenly zinged past Conor's head and he turned, startled, in time to see several creatures in the trees off to the north side of the mound. Creatures were the only way to describe them because they were green and brown, blending in with the foliage like woodland wraiths. They whooped and yelled and threw things, and started dropping out of the trees. When they began to run, Conor could see that they were human; naked human men painted in dirty shades of green and brown.

They clutched crude bows in their hands made of thin, stripped branches and some kind of animal sinew. Conor could hardly believe what he was seeing; it was like watching an ancient reenactment only this one had the distinct element of danger; people didn't launch arrows because they wanted to be friendly. They launched them because they wanted to kill. One of the group launched a very crude arrow again and it weakly sailed off to the left.

As they drew closer, Conor knew the meant to attack them but he still couldn't believe it. He just stood there and observed, like an anthropologist would. Beside him, Destry let out a shriek.

"Holy Crap!" she yelped.

Her cry seemed to startle him from clinically evaluating the situation. Although he was an expert in ancient warfare, he'd never really had cause, other than an occasional bar fight, to use his skills. As big as he was, at six and a half feet tall, he'd never really been called upon to use his hand to hand combat skills in a mortal situation and, truth be told, he was a little frightened. But he could see that all of that was about to change. He was about to put his money where his mouth was. Something in his gut told him that these men were not the reasoning type. They looked like wild animals and he responded in kind.

A fist the size of a ten pound ham came flying out at the first man, delivering a crushing blow that sent him to the ground. Conor grabbed the second man by the neck and tossed him off into the trees. Two others descended on him and he found himself in a vicious fight, tossing men to the ground only to have them jump up and try to strike him. One man had a crude bronze knife blade and he swiped it at Conor, catching him in the arm and drawing blood. Furious, Conor drove his fist into the man's head.

Destry had darted away when Conor threw the first punch; she had nowhere to go and no place to hide, but she didn't want to get clobbered in the fight. She'd never in her life heard of gangs hanging out in the countryside of Ireland, beating up tourists.   But there were at least six of them, three of them who were already out cold thanks to Conor's crushing blows. The man could deliver a punch like nothing she had ever seen this side of a movie screen.   But as she watched him, she began to realize that he might need help. She'd never been in a fight in her life but that was about to change; she had to help him.

Over to her left, the strange woman was trying to get her attention, beckoning her to come, but Destry had no intention of going with the woman or of leaving Conor alone. Forgetting her splitting headache and nausea, she quickly looked around for anything she could use as a weapon. Rocks would do but she quickly spied a fairly thick branch on the ground, about four feet long and with leaves and smaller branches still growing out of it. Swiftly, she retrieved it and the next time one of those skinny naked guys came around, she whacked him over the head with it. He fell like a stone.

This left two men going after Conor; he had one of them in a headlock and the other one by the throat. Destry rushed up with her branch and cracked the guy in the headlock on the back of the head with it. Surprised, Conor looked up just in time to see Destry brain the last man in his grip; she took a swing at his head like a baseball player swinging a bat and knocked the guy out of the park. But he was tough and she had to whack him twice.

When he fell to the ground, unconscious, Conor suddenly let out a roar and beat at his chest, kicking at the men on the ground. It was a release of fear, the expending of testosterone, on the most basic primal level. Destry, sickened by the fight, dropped her branch and staggered back, tripping over a rock and ending up on her bum. There she sat as Conor bellowed his victory.

He was hyped up on adrenalin, the primordial surge of battle in his veins. He was a strong personality as it was, demonstrative, but his victory yell was truly something to behold. For a man who had never truly been in a battle situation, he had taken to it with frightening ease. Still riding the adrenalin high, he looked up from his six victims to see Destry sitting on the ground looking horribly pale. He forgot his testosterone seizures and rushed to her.

"Are you all right?" he reached down to pick her up off the grass. "Did you get hurt?"

She shook her head, weakly trying to pull away from him and struggling to hold back the tears. But the tears came and she broke down.

"I'm fine," she sobbed softly. "I just want to get out of here."

He put his big arms around her, pulling her against him. "I'm sorry; so sorry," he murmured, giving her a gentle squeeze. Putting his enormous arm around her shoulders, he pulled her away from the pile of bodies. "Come on; we'll get out of here right now."

"Who were those guys?" she wept.

He hugged her again, gently. "I don't know, sweetheart," he said. "A group of ruffians; who knows?"

"They don't have any clothes on."

"A group of insane nudists, then. I don't know who they are."

Destry was torn between giggling at his humor and her tears, and the tears won out as he began to walk her in the direction of the car park; or, at least, where the car park had once been. He didn't know what else to do. But Padraigan was still lingering now behind him with her three little helpers, leading the shaggy horses with them.

"Wait," Padraigan called. "Please, my lord, not that way. We must go this way."

He turned to look at the woman, exhaustion evident on his face now that the adrenalin rush was gone. "I'm not going to…."

Destry cut him off. "What does she want?"

He grunted as he turned to look at her. "She wants us to go with her. She insists."

Destry waved him off. "Maybe we should," she said, her gaze on what should be the carpark in the distance. "There's no car out there and now that I look at it, no road. There's no farmhouse or cars driving by or anything else that moves. There's nothing at all. We just got attacked by crazy, dirty naked guys who tried to shoot arrows at us. What in the hell is going on here, anyway?"

His gaze was moving with hers, seeing the same sights, feeling the same dread. "I don't know."

Destry's teary gaze looked up at him. "Maybe she knows."

Conor didn't say anything for a moment. But he came to a stop, his hands still on Destry as he turned for Padraigan. There was suspicion and anxiety in his tone, but considering the circumstances, he figured that he didn't have much choice.

"We will go with you," he told her in her language.

Padraigan smiled timidly, encouraging her little helpers to provide horses to Conor and Destry. Destry had ridden a great deal and mounted easily when Conor gave her a leg up. He, however, took a bit longer; throwing his big body over the back of the horse, he finally swung a leg over and sat up somewhat uncertainly. He didn't look particularly comfortable. But as storm clouds began to gather again over head, he followed Padraigan and her little group off to the east, heading into a massive forest he had never even noticed before, and losing themselves in the dark and musty depths of the thickening trees.

CHAPTER SEVEN

The sense of urgency followed them for a few miles, fearful that they were perhaps being followed by whatever dangers Padraigan had eluded to. Through the trees they moved, sometimes traveling through bramble so thick that the horses had a difficult time getting through it. But Padraigan urged them onward and the little people swatted the horses with switches to get them going. The forest around them was thick and still, the canopy dense, and the feeling of unease pervasive. It was like an impenetrable cloak that none of them could shake, this odd feeling of disorientation and apprehension that seemed to blanket them.

Conor felt it but he didn't say anything to Destry, who finally seemed to be feeling better after their rough experience. She was actually enjoying the horse ride, patting the animal on the neck or stroking its mane. Not being used to horses, however, Conor was more than ready to get off the animal shortly after they started. His bum was killing him, as well as something else a bit more tender, so when they eventually entered a clearing deep in the thick wood and Padraigan dismounted her small white pony, Conor slid off his big shaggy horse and started walking. He just couldn't take riding anymore and rubbed at his backside to bring some circulation into it. He swore it was numb. Beside him and still astride her fat gray beast, Destry grinned down at him.

"Hurt yourself, Dr. Daderga?" she teased.

He gave her his best scowl. "Mind your own business."

For the first time since he'd met her, Destry burst into unrestrained laughter. It was a wonderful sound. "Poor baby," she joked. "Not much of a cowboy, are you?"

He cast her a long look. "I have it on good authority that you're about to be spanked if you don't zip your lips."

She giggled and steered her horse away from him so that there was a good gap in distance. "I'm sorry," she said, although she didn't mean a word of it. She was leaning back to get a good look at his butt beneath the baggy jeans. "I hate to tell you this, but your ass is flat. You must have damaged it riding on the horse."

He just shook his head as he walked, a smile playing on his lips. He wouldn't look at her.

"Great," he said sarcastically, heightening his strong Irish brogue. "Now my ass is damaged. If I had trouble getting you to go out with me before, now I've just lost a one of the biggest guns in my arsenal. What else can I attract you with if not my fantastic, now flattened, ass?"

Destry hooted as the horses plodded along. "How about those fabulous biceps?"

He looked at her, very hopeful. "You like my biceps?"

Her laughter faded and her bright blue eyes twinkled at him. "I do," she admitted. "You must work out diligently."

He snorted. "Religiously," he concurred. "My father was an amateur bodybuilder and he started me when I was in my teens. If I don't maintain this bulk, it turns to fat and then I'll look just like Dowth mound – a big, round blob. So I go to the gym three or four times a week."

"Did you compete as a bodybuilder?"

He shook his head. "No," he replied. "I was more interested in school. My dad was disappointed, too; he doesn't have nearly my height or build and he always wished he had. He used to give me grief about not reaching my potential."

She watched him walk, still rubbing his bum. "You reached your potential academically," she said. "You're a Ph.D., for Heaven's sake; wasn't he proud of you about that?"

He nodded, how watching the ground as it passed beneath his feet. "Sure," he said. "I have a double doctorate in Celtic and Irish History as well as Anthropology, but he would have been proud of me if I ended working at a petrol station."

She smiled, looking away flirtatiously when he glanced over at her. Conor was so smitten with her that it was all he could think about even though they had bigger problems at hand. For the moment, she was responding to him as she never had before and he wanted to enjoy every minute of it. Finally, her walls of defense were cracking and he was banging away at them with a sledgehammer.

"Do you have brothers?" she asked, gazing off into the trees.

He nodded. "One," he replied. "Gerritt is eighteen months younger than I am."

"Any sisters?"

"None," he looked over at her and their eyes met. "You have a sister, right?"

She nodded. "Caitlin."

"Does she look anything like you?"

Her smile was back. "A little," she said. "She's taller than I am. She teaches high school."

"Is she married?"

She laughed softly. "No," she said. "Why? Are you looking for a wife?"

He lifted a red eyebrow. "I've already found one; she just doesn't know it yet."

Destry's smile faded as she stared at him, knowing he meant her. She looked away and Conor could feel the mood plummet. He scrambled to get it back on track.

"Did I do it again?" he asked softly.

She was looking off into the woods. "Do what?"

"Offend you?"

She didn't say anything for a moment. Then she sighed, shaking her head and petting the horse absently. "No," she said after a moment. "It's just that I don't know what to say when you say things like that."

Conor watched her carefully, her body language. He wasn't very good at reading women but he was trying very hard.

"I guess I shouldn't say them at all," he said quietly. "But I can't help myself. Destry, if you're not interested in me in a romantic sense, just say so. I don't want to make you uncomfortable by telling you what's on my mind if it's not something you want to hear."

She looked at him. "That's not the case at all," she suddenly averted her gaze, looking back to the horse again and fiddling with its mane. "Maybe that's the problem. I just feel... confused."

"Why?"

She lifted her shoulders. "Because I was supposed to be married two weeks ago," she paused, thinking of how to voice her thoughts. "You know something? I've done a lot of thinking in that time and I came to realize that I'm really not all that upset about losing Jake. If I really think hard about it, he was a jerk; self-absorbed, mean at times, critical. He was hard to be around. So I guess in that sense I really don't miss the guy. I don't miss the pressure I felt every time he came around me. It seems to me that what I'm most upset about is being humiliated. And that's selfish."

He was watching her intently, gradually walking in her direction and closing the gap between them. "No, it's not," he said somewhat gently. "It's perfectly natural to be upset at being dumped on your wedding day. Don't you love the guy?"

She thought a moment; hard. Then she started to shake her head. "I guess I really don't," she admitted. "Sure, I thought I did at first, but then the infidelity rumors started... oh, hell, I don't know; when we got engaged, it all happened so fast. He's a fairly popular sports figure in the States and I guess I just got swept up in it. I think I was more in love with the idea of getting married than with who I was actually marrying. In hindsight, being left at the altar was probably the best thing that happened to me. I just don't see our marriage lasting."

He stared up at her, finding her confession both interesting and oddly encouraging. "Aisling said he wasn't very nice to you," he said softly.

Destry smiled ironically. "He wasn't," she agreed. "Just little things; you know, not opening a door for me, or pulling out my chair, or telling me he loved me or that I was beautiful. But there were bigger things, too; he'd be out on the road for weeks, come home and spend the night at my house and then take off again for weeks. He rarely called me from the road and when he did, it was always really hurried as if he had better things to do. I think… I think he just used me for sex and the fact that his friends really liked me. I heard his friends say that I made him look good."

She trailed off, falling silent, and Conor noticed that, up ahead, they were coming upon an extremely crude structure. His gaze drifted over the sod construction of the beastly little hut, realizing that it was very primitive. In this day and age, he'd never seen or heard of people still living like this in Ireland, not in the farthest reaches of the isle, and his Anthropologist's brain started kicking in. He was starting to wonder if he hadn't discovered an entirely new Irish culture, something primal and crude right in the midst of modern-day Ireland. His attention was becoming diverted by the new scenery but he retained enough focus to answer her.

"Well," he finally said. "Like I said before, the guy was a moron. You're the most beautiful women in the world and never under any circumstances would I not pull out a chair for you, or open a door, or tell you every day that I loved you. That's what you deserve. You deserve to be treated like a queen."

Destry glanced at him, feeling her heart race a little at his declaration, but she was prevented from replying as Padraigan suddenly headed in their direction, speaking to Conor in that odd dialect. The woman might as well have been speaking Martian for all Destry understood it, so she remained silent while the tiny white woman addressed Conor.

"*An mbeidh tú féin agus an banríon teacht taobh istigh le do thoil?*" she asked. "*Beidh mo sheirbhísigh a réiteach na capaill.*"

"What did she say?" Destry whispered to him.

He handed over the reins to one of the poorly dressed midgets and went over to Destry, reaching up to help her off the horse. "She asked you and me to go inside," he replied. "Her little friends will tend the horses."

Destry slid into his arms and he lowered her to the ground. Padraigan was already up ahead, heading towards the sorry-looking hut, and Conor took Destry's hand in his big palm and began to follow. Destry rather liked the feel of his big, warm hand around hers and didn't pull away. She went right along with it as they made their way across the heavy, wet grass towards the structure almost hidden within a cluster of trees.

Conor looked around the compound with interest; there was a ragged-looking barn for the horses flanked by a giant pile of dried grass. Next to that was a pile of wood and behind that he could see a crudely fashioned corral of sorts that contained two sheep, a goat and a shaggy cow. Everything was run down, cluttered, and crude. As they drew closer to the hut, he could see that it was entirely of sod, built in between two trees that protected it from the elements and also provided a great deal of camouflage. It was primitive and small, and when Padraigan opened the door, he had to fold himself over in order to enter.

Once inside, it smelled of earth and dampness. It was three rooms wide; a main room in the middle flanked by two smaller rooms, all uneven and asymmetrical. The floor was dirt and pitted with small divots. A badly made table sat in the center of the room along with four stools. Padraigan indicated the stools.

"Sit," she invited. "I will start a fire."

Conor still had hold of Destry's hand as he bent over and pulled out a stool for her. She grinned at him as she took it and he pulled out the stool next to her, picking it up to look at it with a critical eye.

"This thing will never hold me," he growled.

Destry grinned, shaking her head. "How much to you weigh?"

He cocked an eyebrow at her. "A lot."

She giggled. "You can't be more than three hundred pounds."

He made a face at her and set the stool down. "About twenty stone, so don't be so smug."

"Convert that into pounds for your American friend."

"About two hundred and seventy pounds."

He was carefully lowering himself onto the stool as she watched. "Well," she sighed. "If it breaks, at least you don't have far to fall to the floor."

"Very funny."

He sat and the stool held, at least for the moment. He was seated right up against Destry, his left thigh and arm against her. She was looking at the stool, grinning up at him when she abruptly noticed the blood on his arm. His jacket was torn and she began to peel it back to get a better look.

"What happened here?" she wanted to know, peeling back the material and noting the big gash on his left forearm. "Ouch. How did you get that?"

He looked down at it. "When those naked guys attacked us," he replied. "One of them had a knife."

She clucked regretfully as she took a closer look. "That may need stitches, Conor. We should get you to an emergency room."

"I'll get it looked at when we get you looked at. How are you feeling?

"Better," she said. "But my head is killing me. I wouldn't be surprised if I have a mild concussion."

"Then we need to get out of here."

She couldn't disagree with him, looking around the dark, crude hut, her gaze falling on the small woman lighting the fire in the tiny hearth. She leaned in to Conor, whispering, as her eyes remained on Padraigan.

"I don't see a phone here," she muttered. "What do we do?"

He wiped at his goatee in a thoughtful, if not nervous, gesture. His eyes were on Padraigan, too.

"I'm not sure we can do anything right now," he leaned over, his lips on her ear. "Just sit tight and we'll figure it out."

There wasn't much more they could do. Sitting silently, Destry felt Conor's arm go around her waist, his hand coming to rest gently on the curve of her torso. Just like the hand-holding a few moments earlier, she didn't try to pull away. He was trying to be casual about it, but there was nothing casual about the man's touch. It was like fire. She let go of her resistance and allowed herself to enjoy it. Feeling his enormous body next to her, warm and protective, brought her tremendous comfort.

When Padraigan finally stood up from the hearth, she turned to the pair with a gentle smile on her face. Behind her, the hearth was sparking and the door opened, emitting one of the little people with wood in his arms. As he fussed with the growing fire, Padraigan went into one of the small adjoining rooms and banged about. Conor and Destry looked at each other, curiously, before the woman emerged with three wooden cups and a pitcher made from some kind of clay.

It was very primitive and Conor's scientist brain kicked in again, visually examining it. Padraigan set the cups down and poured a dark liquid into each of the cups, putting full vessels in front of Destry and Conor. Then she sat on one of the stools and faced them.

"I realize this is all very strange to you," she said, mostly to Conor. "But you must know the truth."

Conor relayed the words to Destry before replying. "What truth?" he asked.

Padraigan lifted her cup, encouraging Destry and Conor to do the same. Conor picked his up immediately but Destry was more hesitant. When he took a big gulp of the liquid, she took a timid sip and nearly choked; it was some kind of very strong alcohol and she sputtered as she set the cup down, wiping the burning liquid from her lips. Conor looked at her and grinned.

"Are you all right?" he asked.

She had her hands around her throat as if she was choking. "Fine," she rasped.

He laughed softly, the hand on her waist moving to pat her on the back gently as she sputtered. He was about to say something more to her when Padraigan interrupted.

"Although you do not remember now, in time, it will come to you," she said to Conor. Then her gaze traveled back and forth between the Conor and Destry, seeing two people she had known very well, once. She knew this day would come; it was crucial for her to make them understand what had happened or all would be lost. "Your name is Conor mac Aonghusa, oidhre chun an throne ard. You are a great king, my lord, Conor ard rí Ciannachta, so great that your legacy is already established and you are much admired and much feared throughout Ireland. The woman at your side is Etain, your queen, and the two of you have three sons together; Mattock, Devlin and Slane."

Conor stared at the woman, hearing her words but beyond that, he wasn't comprehending much. He was still fixated on the first sentence of her story.

"'Conor, son of Aengus, heir to the high *throne*'?" he repeated, almost in disgust. "Where did you get that? What in the hell is that?"

Padraigan remained calm. "Please, my lord, hear me," she begged. "Your legacy as a ruler and warrior is so great that your brother, a vain and jealous man, began to want for the throne himself. He made a few attempts on your life but you were too clever for him. You evaded him at every turn and eventually, you banished him from your kingdom. But your brother dabbles in the dark arts, my lord; he lured you to a conference under the guise of peace and commanded his sorcerer, Olc of the Eye, to exile you into the dark mists of the nether regions. As soon as we realized this had happened, your wife sent your children into safe hiding with me. Then she took your army and went to your brother to demand your safe return, but your brother tricked her into a private meeting and his sorcerer exiled her as well. You were both sent through the doras ama, to the same nether region. But your brother, fearful that you would someday return to kill him, cast a curse upon you; you and you wife would have no memory of each other and no memory of the life you shared. You would wander in the nether region forever, ignorant of who you really were and of your mighty kingdom."

Conor gaped at the woman as if she had lost her mind. After several moments of staring, he wiped at his goatee again in an inherently nervous gesture, and simply shook his head.

"That's madness," he hissed. "You're mad."

Padraigan shook her head. "Nay, my lord, on either account," she said softly. "I knew what Olc had done to you; he had sent you and your wife through the doras ama at a time where the day and night are of the same.

At the moment where day turns into night, the door opens to the nether regions and for a brief moment, we may see both worlds through the swirling mists. I traveled to the sacred mound when I knew this time was approaching, many times since Olc banished you both, and was able to see your wife at my most recent visit. I spoke to her, hoping she would return, and she did. She heard me and she returned. *Fanacht, morrigan, gnáthlá agus oiche og ceanna; tar ar cúl do sinne.*"

As Conor sat, dumbfounded and apprehensive, Destry finally spoke up. She put her hand on his enormous thigh to get his attention. "There's that phrase again," she squeezed his leg until he looked at her. She looked rather frightened. "That's the woman who spoke to me from the tunnels, isn't it?"

He stared at her, hardly believing what he was hearing. But as he gazed into her bright blue eyes, studying her, Padraigan's bizarre story suddenly started making some sense. He remembered the first time he had seen Destry; he couldn't take his eyes off her. He said once that an angel had walked into his midst and that's exactly what it had felt like. Her lure to him had almost been magnetic, it had been so strong. Even as he gazed at her now, it was the most natural of things being with her, as if they were meant to be together in every way. He couldn't explain it better than that.

Conor exhaled heavily, rubbing at his forehead as his brain tried to process what he was being told. At some point, Destry was going to want to know what Padraigan was telling him. He didn't want to answer her now because he didn't have any answers himself. His gaze moved back to the tiny, wispy woman.

"Those mounds are burial chambers from long ago," he told her. "They're not doorways to the nether region."

Padraigan lifted an eyebrow. "They were not built by men," she said. "They were built by gods. When the sun is just so, the doorway opens. It opened today when you and your queen stepped through. I called to you and you came."

Destry squeezed his thigh again but he put a big hand over hers, stilling it. He wanted to make sure he was absolutely clear on things before he started translating because, quite honestly, he was rather overwhelmed by it all. It was crazy, interesting and oddly believable all at the same time. He looked at Padraigan with a mixture of suspicion, disbelief and fear.

"None of that makes any sense," he told her. "Destry is not my wife. I only just met her. And we have lives; I remember where I was born and I know my parents. How do you explain that?"

Padraigan lifted her slender shoulders. "Rebirth."

His brow furrowed. "Rebirth? What does that mean?"

"It means that your transition into the nether region saw you reborn," she murmured. "You returned as an infant and grew into the man you are today. That is why you only remember your life in the nether region. But you are still our king; you are still Conor ard rí Ciannachta, and we need you here."

He just stared at her, hard. "Conor, High King of Ciannachta," he translated softly. He had to admit, he liked the ring of it. But that didn't dispel the fact that it was nonsense; his logical mind just couldn't give in, not yet. "I'm not a high king. I'm not anything. You must have me mixed up with someone else."

She smiled faintly. "May I ask a question, my lord?"

"Go ahead."

"How do you explain your appearance outside of the doras ama? You said yourself that nothing looks as you remember it. Would the nether region change so much in the blink of an eye that you would not recognize it?"

He sat back, regarding her, trying to come up with an answer that would satisfy them both, mostly because he was feeling a great deal of horror in the realization that any answer he could come up with lent credence to her story. But something in his brain, some small and tucked away place, was telling him that what the woman said just might be true. It was more a feeling than anything else and he was resistant to it. But that resistance was fading.

"It's a great story, I'll give you that," he put up a hand as if to block her out. "And I appreciate your hospitality. But Destry and I need to get to a hospital. If you don't have a phone we can use, do you have any neighbors with phones?"

Padraigan's gaze was steady. "If I can prove to you that what I say is true, will you believe?"

He lifted his eyebrows and scratched at his head, showing signs of restlessness and exasperation. "Sure," he said. "Go ahead. Do your worst."

Padraigan stood up and disappeared into the small room where she had retrieved the cups and pitcher. When she vanished from view, Destry turned to Conor and squeezed his big thigh again.

"Now will you tell me what she said?" she hissed.

He nodded his head, putting his arm around her shoulders to calm her down. "I think she's nuts."

"Really? Why?"

He sighed and looked her in the eye, trying to summarize what he was told and not flip her out in the process. "Well," he scratched at his goatee. "She says that Dowth is apparently not so much a Neolithic burial chamber as it is some kind of time-travel device. She says that I am really some kind of high king and you are really my wife. Evidently I have a jealous brother who had his wicked sorcerer banish us into whatever doorway opens up in Dowth, sending us into the nether region with no memory of our former life or of each other. She further says that she called to you and that you heeded her call. That was the voice you heard calling to you in your dreams."

Destry stared at him as he finished his tale. He could see the thought processes in her expression; interest to incredulity to disbelief. By the time he was finished, however, her cheeks were growing pink and he could see tears in her eyes.

"I *did* hear her voice," she hissed, leaping up from the stool. "I told you I heard her voice. But she must have been lying in wait for me somehow, hiding in those old tunnels."

"What about the dreams?"

She looked increasingly upset. "She must have freaked me out so bad with her whispers in the tunnel that I just dreamed of them," she insisted. "Maybe she hypnotized me; I just don't know. How else can you explain something like that?"

"You heard two complete phrases."

"Whose side are you on?"

He could see how upset she was becoming and he grasped her hands to keep her from panicking. "Your side," he insisted softly. "I'm always on your side."

"Let's get out of here before something awful happens."

He nodded patiently. "We'll leave," he assured her. "But I need you to calm down, sweetheart. There's no reason to get so upset."

"So upset?" she repeated, her voice rising in pitch. "That woman is telling you crazy stories and you just sit here calmly listening to them."

"You're the one that said we needed to come with her."

She shook her head so hard that her long hair flopped in her eyes. "I've changed my mind," she said. "We need to leave before she murders us. She's set us up somehow. I want to go back to the hotel now."

He put up a hand to soothe her before she went wild. "We'll go," he murmured, trying to steer her back onto her stool. "Just calm down. Please."

She opened her mouth to argue with him when Padraigan entered the room again, followed by her three little helpers. Her gaze moved between Destry, standing up and looking at her with some fear, and Conor as he held on to Destry's hands. Padraigan could guess what had happen by the skittish look on Destry's face. When she spoke, it was mostly directed at Destry.

"My great and noble queen," she said softy. "Do you not recognize my face? You and I were as sisters, once."

Conor looked up to Destry and quietly relayed the question. Destry shook her head fearfully in response and Padraigan continued.

"Your love for your husband was great," she told the story with a delicate lilt. "So strong it was that it could move mountains. You and the king loved each other from times of old, from times before this, passing through the centuries in different forms but with the same strong love for one another. Somehow, you always found each other no matter what. And it is your love for your husband, and for your family, that gives you your strength. It binds you, protects you and guides you. It is that love that has guided you here today."

Conor whispered Padraigan's words to Destry verbatim. Confused, frightened, Destry didn't have any reply other than to burst into quiet tears. Conor gently pulled her down onto his lap, wrapping his enormous arms around her and hugging her. He didn't know what else to do. Padraigan took a few timid steps towards the couple, her tender focus on Destry.

"When Olc of the Eye exiled your husband through the *doras ama*, you came to me with one request," she whispered. "You wanted me to protect your sons, three fine, strong lads in the image of their father. Of course I agreed and it is since that time that I have lived out here in the wilds, concealing the lads from those who would harm them. Today I will give them back to you and then you will understand the truth of my words."

Conor's gaze lingered on Padraigan a moment before he reluctantly relayed the statement to Destry. Her weeping grew stronger and she wrapped her arms around his neck, burying her face against his shoulder. It was as if she was trying to hide. He held her tightly, his gaze riveted to Padraigan, wondering with some trepidation what she was going to do next.

The wispy woman met Conor's gaze strongly before turning to the hearth. There was a clutter of containers and other miscellaneous vials near one corner of the hearth, lined up against the stone of the wall, and she began rummaging about in the clutter. Pulling forth a wooden vessel, she blew the dust out of it and began to pour various ingredients into it.

"When you brought your sons to me for safe keeping, I knew that it would be a difficult task to hide them against those who would seek to harm them," she said, pouring another measure of something mysterious into the cup and swirling the contents. "I also knew that I could not keep them locked in a hole until your return, so the most logical conclusion I could reach was to hide them in plain sight. And they have been hidden, in full view, since your exile."

She poured a final ingredient into the cup and watched it smoke. By this time, Destry had calmed her tears and was watching the woman mix the concoction. But her arms were still wrapped around Conor's neck, holding on to him tightly.

"What's she saying?" she sniffled.

He turned to look at her, his face right up against hers. He couldn't help himself from kissing her on the cheek.

"She says that when you brought our sons to her for safe keeping, she had to hide them in plain sight," he said softly.

Destry turned to look at him, realizing she was literally right up against his face. She loosened her grip on his neck slightly, just enough so there was a few inches of space between them. But she found herself giving in to the closeness, feeling the heat from the man's body and loving it. He was so powerful, so sweet and compassionate, that she could feel herself succumbing to it.

Truth be told, she really didn't care any longer. She didn't care that she'd had a broken engagement two weeks ago or confusion about her love life and her future. There was something about Conor Daderga that broke down her walls and touched her deeply.

She lifted an eyebrow at him. "You know," she murmured thoughtfully. "If you and I had… well, you know… I think I would have remembered it."

He smiled. "I know for a fact that I would have."

"She says we have children together?"

"That's what she says."

"I think I would have remembered giving birth, too."

He laughed softly. "I would remember that also. It wouldn't be like me to forget my baby's mama."

She started laughing. "You sound like you've had experience with that kind of thing."

He snorted. "Thank God, no," he said. "I'm just saying that I think I would have remembered the woman who gave birth to my children."

Destry gazed into his sky blue eyes, permitting herself for the first time to feel the pull between them. She didn't resist. "I don't think it would be such a bad thing to give birth to your children," she murmured. "I'll bet you'd make a great dad."

He couldn't help it; he leaned forward and slanted his lips over hers, kissing her gently and passionately. Destry wrapped her arms tightly around his neck and kissed him in return, the first time she voluntarily did so. It was warm, gently, but full of promise. Thrilled, Conor was preparing to deliver a more powerful kiss in response but Padraigan's voice interrupted his intentions.

"Mattock is your eldest and a very good lad," she stood up from her make-shift laboratory. "He took the potion first. When Devlin and Slane saw Mattock drink it, they took it as well. The spell transformed the boys into dwarves so they would not be suspected by those intent to harm them."

She was moving to the three dwarves standing expectantly behind her. She handed the cup to the first little man and he took two big, healthy swallows. Then she passed it to the other two, who drained it between them. Setting the cup down, Padraigan stood back and watched.

Conor and Destry were watching, too. The three little men seemed to stand there for a small eternity, looking at each other, inspecting their hands, touching their faces. Then, the first dwarf who had drank the potion suddenly coughed loudly and fell back onto his bum. He groaned and flipped over onto his belly, kicking his legs and mumbling unintelligible words. Concerned and curious, Destry and Conor strained to catch a glimpse of what was going on when the other two little men went down.

Being a nurse, Destry's first instinct was to help. She stood up from Conor's lap, trying to get a better look at the writhing men.

"What did she give them?" she demanded, looking at Conor. "Ask her what she gave them."

Conor said something to Padraigan, who merely turned to smile at him. Destry, increasingly concerned as the three little men rolled around on the dirt floor and grunted, tried to move towards them but Conor stopped her. He had hold of her hand, pulling her back towards him.

"Wait a minute," he said softly. "I doubt she's poisoned them right in front of us. Just wait and see what happens."

She still wasn't convinced. "But they're obviously in distress," she said. "At least let me take a look at them and make sure their vital signs are strong."

He could see the feet of the little men as they rolled around, the backside of their bodies, but not much else. He finally shook his head. "If something is going on, I don't want you to get caught up in it," he said. "You've already got a mild concussion and I don't want to see something worse happen to you. Just... give this a moment to see what happens, okay? If it looks like they're getting worse, then you can take a look."

Torn, concerned, Destry did as he asked although she wasn't completely comfortable with it. She let him pull her back down onto his lap, his big arms winding around her torso again. But as she watched, something strange began to happen.

First, she thought it was a trick of the light. She began to see an odd aura around the men, something that looked slightly purple. She blinked her eyes but it didn't go away. Then she rubbed at her eyes but it still didn't go away. As she watched, the first little man pushed himself to his knees. The purple light around him undulated, seemingly transforming him like a hand would transform clay. The man's body moved strangely, elongating, working with the tricks of the light to transform him into something taller and more slender. By the time the man stood up, he wasn't anything as he had been. Whatever magic the light accomplished was evident in the younger, taller and skinnier figure. He was no longer writhing or grunting, now completely calm as the purple aura faded. Then he turned around.

The man was no longer a man; he was a boy, perhaps eight or ten years of age, with auburn hair and bright blue eyes. He was a handsome child with beautiful features, his gaze moving immediately to Destry and Conor. His gaze met with two pairs of startled eyes, inquisitive, then joyful. Suddenly, he was bolting across the floor and throwing himself into Destry's lap.

Destry shrieked when the boy landed in her lap, his arms around her and Conor, his little face pressed into her belly.

"*Máthair, athair!*" the child cried. "*Tá mé caillte agat!*"

Destry had her hands full of little boy. "What did he say?" she asked Conor.

Conor, too, was looking with astonishment at the boy on Destry's lap. "He called us mother and father," he said. "He said that he has missed us."

Destry looked at Conor, her eyes wide with bewilderment. "He thinks we're his...?"

She didn't get a chance to finish her sentence; suddenly, two more boys were rushing at them, both with light brown hair, about six and four years of age, respectively. They threw themselves on top of the other boy, now all three young lads squirming in Destry's lap. They were weeping with joy, especially the little one; he was an adorable little boy with light brown hair and sky blue eyes. When he gazed up at Destry, tears running down his face, she felt the overwhelming need to pick him up and hold him. She had no idea who the kid was but that didn't matter; he was distressed and she wanted to comfort him. The child wrapped himself up around her, holding her tightly, as she looked at Conor.

There were tears in her eyes. "These poor little boys," she whispered as tears trickled down her face. "They're so... sad."

Conor had his lap full with Destry and the other two boys. He, too, felt the instinct to comfort them. It was true that they were distraught but there was also something else deep in his heart that cried out to these children. The sensation confused and distressed him as a big hand found its way onto the oldest boy, still weeping in his lap. The child's head came up and he threw his arms around Conor's neck, holding the man tightly.

"*Athair*," he squeezed Conor's neck. "You have come home. You have come back!"

Conor hesitantly hugged the boy, not knowing what else to do. He looked at Destry over the top of the auburn head, their eyes meeting and silent words of bewilderment and compassion passing between them. It would seem that neither one of them knew what to do about these children. But Destry seemed a little more edgy, more fearful.

"Those… those midgets were really these children," she breathed.

Conor lifted his eyebrows reluctantly. "I suppose so," he muttered. "I just don't know. There has to be a logical explanation for it."

"Like what?" she wanted to know, whispering desperately. "You saw them turn into these kids just like I did. What's logical about that?"

She was growing agitated, even with the four year old child wrapped up around her. Conor simply didn't have an answer for her. "I don't know," he wouldn't look at her. "But there has to be some kind of explanation."

Destry's gaze drifted to the biggest lad, the one with his face pressed into Conor's neck. She studied the child, the shape of his head, and began to feel the faint wafts of déjà vu clutching at her. The feeling got stronger the more she stared at the child; more than that, the feel of the little one in her arms was vague familiar, as if she had known it once before. It was the sweetest thing she could have imagined. Her gaze found Conor once again.

"Did you see his face?" she whispered. "Conor, he looks just like you."

Conor hadn't gotten a good look; now he wasn't sure he wanted to. So much of this situation was now becoming unbearably real to him and he felt like he was losing his grip on what he believed to be his reality. After a moment, he held the boy back, at arm's length, and studied his handsome little face. He found himself inspecting bright blue eyes that looked just like Destry's, and a mouth, nose and jaw line that looked just like his. It was the weirdest thing he had ever seen.

"*Cad é do ainm, buachaill?*" he asked softly.

What's your name, boy? The lad looked as if he was about to weep with joy. "Mattock," he responded. "I love you, Dada. I missed you."

Conor didn't know what to say; the little boy was so sad, so pathetic, he couldn't help but hug the child. He just didn't know what else to do. He looked over at Destry, who had her face buried in the top of the four-year-old's head. As he watched, the middle boy cuddled up against her and she opened one of her arms for him, holding him tightly. He had to admit, as he watched the scene, that something inside him felt whole and settled. It was the most overwhelmingly comforting feeling he had ever known, as if now he was suddenly and finally complete.

As he watched Destry with the other two boys, pictures began to flash in his mind, like snippets of a movie reel. He saw himself with his hand on a pregnant belly, with a baby in his arms, and then flashes of more children at his feet. He blinked his eyes, shaking his head, thinking he was having hallucinations, but more visions flashed in front of him, this time of Destry. He had visions of kissing her, of making love to her, and he suddenly felt as if his heart was going to explode from his chest from the love he felt for her. He couldn't breathe. All he could feel was adoration that went beyond words, beyond time. He couldn't seem to think or feel anything else.

As Conor struggled through intense visions, Destry was quickly succumbing to something even more intense. The feel and smell of the boys in her arms was doing something to her; somehow, she knew these children. She could feel them deep down in her heart and as she hugged the littlest one, she, too, began to have flashbacks of something fluid and dream-like. She saw Conor in a way she'd never seen him before; dressed in leather, with primitive weapons, and she began to feel such love and affection for the man that she audibly gasped. Then she saw him making love to her and she could feel her limbs grow warm and weak, tasting his kisses and feeling the emotion that he stirred within her.

Flashes of a rounded belly came to her mind, startling her, then finally the last few moments of childbirth as pain surged and she pushed out a male child, who was immediately handed over to a weeping Conor. Tears came to her eyes as she saw these things and felt the powerful emotions they created. But another vision came along, more powerful than the rest, and she was lying on a bed struggling to give birth to another child, pain as she had never experienced surging through her body. It was enough to cause her to release the four year old, setting him down with shaky arms as she stood up, hand to her head as if to forcibly wipe away the visions that were now slamming into her with painful force.

She stood up, hand to her belly, hearing Conor's voice ringing in her head, calling to her, but unable to discern if he was really speaking to her or if it was the odd hallucinations calling out. The vision of childbirth had not gone away; it was more intense now as she envisioned herself pushing out a dead child, hearing someone say that the daughter was not meant to be.

Grief, the depths of which she could have never imagined, swept her and she began crying aloud. She felt pain such as she had never known and her head began to swim. She tried to turn around, to say something to Conor, but she couldn't seem to manage it.

Blackness closed in over her before she realized it.

CHAPTER EIGHT

Conor sat at the table and watched the boys as they moved around the small, mud hut at Padraigan's direction. They had brought him a cup of strong, tart wine, some kind of rustic soda bread, and big hunks of white cheese. The two older boys were obedient and intelligent from what he could see but the youngest didn't want to work. He remained by Destry as the woman lay passed out on a small bed in the next room. The little one hadn't moved from her side.

Conor had carried Destry into the room when she had fainted. Laying her upon the misshapen bed made from branches covered over with a rough blanket, he could only feel great confusion and great remorse as he gazed at her. Her pulse was strong and her breathing regular, so he could only assume that the stress of the situation must have somehow pushed her beyond her endurance. Coupled with everything else she'd gone through over the past two weeks, unconsciousness was her body's way of coping with the stress.

So he kissed her forehead and returned to the bigger room when Padraigan insisted there was nothing they could do for the lady that rest would not more ably accomplish. He sat where he could watch Destry and the youngest boy as he sat by her side, holding her hand and speaking to her in his soft Celtic lilt. The more he observed, the stronger the sense of déjà vu he felt. Every time he looked at the three boys, it was as if something deep inside was struggling to burst forth with recollections. He couldn't quite put his finger on how he knew these children, only that for some reason, he knew he did. And the fact that they looked like him and Destry only fed his sense of confusion and frustration. Something was happening here that he had yet to fully figure out. But, given time, he knew he would. It would come to him.

Padraigan seemed to steer clear of him since her initial tales of his true identity. She sent the boys to gather wood as she went outside and killed a chicken herself. Conor sat in relative silence, watching Destry in one room while inevitably finding interest in Padraigan and her very archaic ways. Her hut was incredibly primitive with no running water, no bathroom that he could see, and its dirt floor and crude furniture. More and more, he was coming to realize that perhaps there was something to what she had told him. Perhaps a door really had opened into the past and he and Destry had really stepped through. He was starting to feel as if there was no other possible explanation for what had happened.

Still, there was a part of his brain, the logical part, that resisted. As the sun began to set and darkness settled over the land, he was starting to feel a new sense of disorientation. To see this primitive land in the daylight was one thing, but when night settled, it was if someone had thrown a black curtain. He'd never seen such darkness. But taking a few steps outside to gaze up at the stars, he couldn't ever remember seeing such a clear dusting of stars. In all his years in Dublin, he'd never seen such a crystal night sky. It was quite beautiful.

Standing just outside the door, he could smell something cooking. Padraigan was making something with the chicken she had killed and he could see the boys off in the crude barn tending to the animals for the night. He was coming to suspect that Padraigan must have said something to the boys about him and Destry, because after their initial display of affection, they had kept a distance. All except for the littlest one; he was still inside seated on the floor next to Destry.

Conor turned to catch a glimpse of her as she lay inside on the small bed. She was still on her side, still passed out. The little boy with the light brown hair was also sleeping now, his head on the bed next to Destry while his body remained on the floor. It was rather touching and Conor smiled faintly at the sight. The little one was a cute kid, no doubt. He couldn't help but warm to the boy.

As he gazed into the warm, fragrant hut, he suddenly realized he had company. He turned to see the two older boys standing next to him, one with a pony on a lead. The boys gazed up at him, timidly.

"Dada," the oldest boy said. "Would you like to see my horse?"

Conor gazed at the boy. "You're Mattock, right?" he asked, watching the boy nod. Then he looked to the middle boy. "What's your name, lad?"

The boy cocked his head as if hurt by the question. "Devlin," he said. "I'm your Devlin."

Conor nodded faintly, realizing that the boy looked a great deal like Destry. He had her bright blue eyes and the shape of her mouth. It was such an odd realization but not an unpleasant one. He had seen the transformation this afternoon just as Destry did, when the dwarves had somehow turned into these young boys. That event, more than anything else, was breaking down his resistance. Something like that just couldn't be explained, even to a man as logical as he was. The longer he looked at the boys, the more he realized that they looked vaguely familiar to him. He felt something for them, kindness and warmth and something else he couldn't put his finger on. He realized that the ideas of these boys as his sons didn't distress him in the least.

He crouched down in front of the boys so he could be more at their level. The two little faces gazed back at him eagerly. Conor looked between them, his gaze both friendly and suspicious.

"You say that you're my Devlin?" he asked the lad with the beautiful auburn hair. "How old are you?"

"I have seen eight years," the boy replied. "I was only seven years when last you saw me. I have grown a whole year."

He said it proudly and Conor fought off a smile. "Then maybe that's why I didn't recognize you," he watched the boy beam from ear to ear. He turned to Mattock. "And you; how old are you?"

Mattock would not be outdone by his brother. "I am eleven years, Dada," he said. "I was only ten years when last you saw me. Have I grown much as well?"

Conor's smile broke through. "You're the biggest boy I've ever seen," he said, watching the boy grin. "I would never have known you. And... and your little brother in there. What's his name?"

Mattock and Devlin looked into the open doorway of the hut. "That is Slane," Mattock replied. "He is just a baby. He was only three when you last saw him. He has cried for Mother every day."

Conor's smile faded as he, too, looked inside to see the little boy sleeping next to Destry. It was touching and sad, and the sight tugged at his heart. With a faint sigh, Conor rose to his full height, towering over the boys, looking between them and feeling his sense of déjà vu grow stronger. He swore he knew these kids. More and more, he could feel it. Moving towards Mattock, he clapped the lad on the shoulder as he pretended to inspect the pony.

"So this is your horse, is it?" he asked. "He's good-looking. What's his name?"

"Deneb," Mattock said proudly. "I can ride him like a warrior."

"How is that?"

Before Mattock could reply, Devlin shoved him. "He still falls off," he announced.

Mattock came back with a balled fist but Conor stopped the slugging before it could start. "Tell me about home, Mattock," he diverted their attention. "When did you last see me?"

As he hoped, the boys were sidetracked. "At Cian," Mattock said. "You were off to fight Geric and Mother begged you not to go. But you did and... well, we did not see you again. Padraigan came for us and brought us here. She made magic upon us and we became *daoine*."

Conor cocked his head. "Little people? Dwarfs?"

Mattock nodded solemnly. "So Geric could not find us."

Conor shook his head in puzzlement. "Who's Geric?"

"Your brother," Padraigan approached; she had been listening just inside the doorway and thought perhaps that now was the time to continue their conversation from earlier in the day. Conor seemed more receptive to it than Destry did and it was imperative for their own safety that they know the entire story. "Geric is your younger brother, my lord. He is the one who ordered Olc of the Eye to banish you and your wife to the Netherworld."

Conor focused on the woman, realizing he wanted to know all of it. Too much about this situation was bizarre; bizarre enough that he was just coming to believe it. It was time he heard everything.

"All right," he rested his fists on his hips, a gesture of resignation. "So I have a brother who had me banished into some magical other-region. If that's true, why did he do it?"

Padraigan's pale eyes were intense. "Your brother is wicked, my lord," she told him. "He has always coveted your kingdom and your abilities as a powerful warrior and a good king. He is an immoral and bitter man and managed to raise a small army to challenge you. You were able to quash him quite easily but he continued to make trouble for you. Then, one day, he asked you to attend a private peace conference and you agreed. When you arrived, without your warrior trappings or your guards, he set Olc upon you and banished you through the *doras amas*. Then he came to your wife to claim her as his own but she escaped him and came to me, begging me to protect your children. As I escaped with the young ones and your court fled for their lives, your brother found your wife again and gave her a choice; either marry him and retain her life as a trusted queen or be banished to the nether region with you. She chose to go with you."

By this time, Conor was feeling a good deal of apprehension and sorrow. He couldn't explain the feelings, only that they were very real. It was as everything she was telling him was saturating his heart, his mind, and he was feeling the story as well as hearing it. It sounded familiar. It felt real.

"So she made the choice to come with me rather than stay with him?" he reiterated. "If that's true and that woman in there is my wife, then why don't I know her?"

Padraigan emphasized her words with her tiny hands. "It was part of the curse that Olc of the Eye cast upon you," she reminded him. "Your curse was to walk the nether world with no knowledge of who you are or who she is. I was able to at least coax you back to the *doras amas* and bring you back where you belong. Now you must remember your place, my lord, and assume your destiny as a mighty king for the sake of your family and your kingdom. We have waited a long time for your return, my lord. You must try hard to remember who you are."

Conor stared at the woman, thinking on her words. He did as she asked; he was trying hard to remember. As crazy as her story sounded, he was aware that he could easily believe it. Something deep inside of him very much wanted to.

"Tell me about my kingdom," he asked. "Maybe that will help."

Padraigan complied. "You are Conor, High King of Ciannachta, and your fortress is Castle Cian along the River Boyne," she said quietly. "You have a mighty army that is loyal to you; they hate your brother because he has formed an unholy alliance with the Northmen who raid this coast. They give him power and money, and in return he allows them access to a great part of Ireland through the river and harbor. The Northmen have killed and plundered many towns because of your brother's alliance with them. For many years, the Northmen would not dare attack Ciannachta because they feared you. You kept our land safe. But your brother has turned all of Ciannachta into a whore for the Northmen, to appease their lust for our riches."

Conor stared at her, digesting what he had been told. Ciannachta. He knew that name, that kingdom. It was the ancient name for Drogheda. Torn between shock, disbelief and something that felt like excitement, his focus turned to the gist of her distress, something that had plagued Ireland, England and Scotland for hundreds of years.

"Northmen?" he repeated. "Viking raiders?"

"Aye, my lord."

"What year is this?"

He didn't really expect that she would know but he asked anyway. Whatever year it was, it had to be well before the Norman conquest of England and the subsequent conquest of Ireland. The Viking raids on Ireland had gone on for hundreds of years so he wasn't sure he could pinpoint when, exactly, this was. But he was determined to try.

Padraigan replied without hesitation. "The Year of the Brown Rabbit."

Conor thought hard on that, knowing that the ancient Irish would measure their time by events, animals or even kings. Try as he might, however, he couldn't seem to remember anything about the year of the brown rabbit that seemed to be significant. So he tried again.

"Who is the king of Dublin?" he asked.

"Gofraid, my lord."

He stared at her. It was name he knew and a history he knew all too well. As he struggled to wrap his mind around the possibility, Padraigan interrupted his turbulent thoughts.

"Please," her tone was reduced to begging. "We need you, my lord. The army hates Geric but they have no choice to serve him because he is king. But let them see their true king and you shall once again have their support and rule of Ciannachta. The army will follow you to the depths of hell if you wished it, my lord. We need you to make us whole and strong again."

Conor's gaze was riveted to the woman, feeling overwhelmed by her tale. But, oddly enough, he didn't resist it. Even as she told him, he felt as if he already knew the details. It was the strangest thing he had ever experienced but even as he rolled the tale over in his mind, the details seemed to make him feel whole, completed. He began to feel strong again.

Behind him, he suddenly heard a noise and turned to see Destry standing in the open doorway. The light from the hut backlit her as she stood there, creating an ethereal vision as the darkness of the night enfolded everything it touched. Destry had little Slane with her, holding the child's hand as her bright blue gaze lingered on Conor.

She looked weary and pale, but in spite of that, Conor had never seen such a beautiful woman. Every time he looked at her, he felt more strongly about her. His heart softened and he began to walk towards her.

"So you're awake," he said gently. "How do you feel?"

She watched him approach. "Better," she said softly. "What was she telling you?"

He stopped when he came upon her, standing just a few inches from her. His dark blue gaze was soft and gentle as he gazed down into her lovely face.

"About my brother and my kingdom," he said quietly. "Or at least what she believes is my brother and my kingdom."

Destry's gaze drifted to Padraigan and then to Slane, still holding her hand. She sighed, still looking at the sweet little boy. "This is just a wild stab in the dark, but I'm guessing that we aren't going back to the hotel."

He wasn't sure how to answer her except with what he believed to be the truth. "No," he murmured. "I don't think there is a hotel."

"Then you really think we passed through some kind of time portal?"

He sighed and put a big hand on her head, pulling her forehead to his lips for a gentle kiss. "Something happened," he muttered. "Until we can figure out what it is, then all we can do is go on the assumption that somehow, some way, we moved back in time."

She looked up at him, her gaze lingering on his handsome face. "So you're supposed to be some sort of king?"

He shrugged. "That's what I'm told. And you're my queen."

She wriggled her eyebrows. "We have three boys."

His dark blue eyes twinkled. "That means that we've...."

She fought off a grin. "I still don't remember that part of it, but I did have weird dreams about giving birth." She looked down at Slane, who was gazing up at her adoringly. She smiled at him as she looked up again, her gaze finding Padraigan. "I had a dream about giving birth to a girl."

Padraigan didn't understand her words so Conor relayed the statement. Padraigan's features gentled. "You did," the sorceress said softly. "Between Devlin and Slane you gave birth to a daughter who was born dead. You named her Angel because you said she was an angel on earth."

Conor whispered the translation and Destry's heart started to beat faster as tears sprang to her eyes. Powerful emotions she didn't recognize, yet somehow remembered, flooded her. She blinked rapidly, chasing away the tears.

"I have a sister named Angel," she whispered.

With Conor translating, Padraigan smiled. "Your Angel found you in the nether region and was reborn as your sister," she assured her. "It is the way of the Life Cycle; our souls find one another in both life and death. Dying never truly separates us from those we love; we all find one another again, eventually."

Conor repeated her answer verbatim and Destry struggled not to burst into tears at the thought. Her dreams were very vivid about giving birth to her children, including her dead daughter. She had visions of Conor weeping over the dead child, so very distraught by the passing.

More than anything, her visions and dreams had conveyed to her the compassion and caring of Conor, a man she had only just met but a man she apparently knew very, very well. Every moment that passed saw her come to know him even better. She was starting to understand just how deeply he was engrained within her. Gazing down at Slane, she squeezed the child's hand before looking back at Conor.

"These children are ours, Conor," she whispered. "I don't have any recollection of being a queen, or of this life we had together, but I can tell you for a fact that these children are ours. I know my children."

He could see that she was deadly serious. He moved closer to her so their bodies were touching, a hand coming up to gently rest on her back, perhaps pulling her a little closer.

"You don't remember me?" he whispered. "I'm told you gave up everything to follow me when I was exiled. I'm told you loved me very much."

The heat from his body was making it difficult for her to breathe. Her head hurt and her stomach was uneasy, but Conor's touch and his closeness seemed to make her forget everything. Her free hand came up and she snaked it around his slender waist, her hand on his back, feeling his warmth and power against the palm. Her heart began to race again, now for an entirely different reason.

"That's possible," she murmured, laying her cheek against his warm, broad chest. He felt incredibly good. "I'm sure you're going to do your best to remind me."

He grinned, both arms going around her to pull her closer. "Absolutely."

She couldn't help but grin at the enthusiastic way in which he said it. She lifted her head to look at him, flicking her eyes leadingly in the direction of the four-year-old at her side. "Everything? Even…?"

He laughed softly. "Especially that."

She joined in his laughter. "I'm not quite sure what to say."

"Say you'll at least give me the chance."

Her laughter faded as she gazed steadily at him. The man's power, his handsome face and his decent character had her spellbound. She could no longer resist him.

"I'll give you the chance," she whispered.

His smile faded, the dark blue eyes roaring with interest and adoration and passion. He didn't miss the fact that she had just given him the green light to pursue her and he was thrilled beyond words. Just as he lost himself in her eyes, preparing to swoop in for a deep and luscious kiss, Mattock's pony suddenly let out a chilling scream.

Everyone jumped at the sound, turning to see the pony being dragged off in the darkness by one leg. Conor watched in shock for a split second before rushing forward to grab Mattock and Devlin, who were rooted to the spot, yelling in fright at the top of their lungs. He thrust the boys in the direction of the mud hut, moving to shove Destry as well but realizing she already had Slane in-hand and was running towards the door. Padraigan scattered but Conor couldn't worry about the woman; he was more concerned with getting Destry and the boys to safety.

Destry couldn't see what had the pony in its grip but she could hear growling and snorting, which scared her to death. Instinct had her practically tossing Slane into the mud hut then pausing at the door as Mattock, Devlin and Conor brought up the rear. She grabbed hold of Mattock and Devlin as they rushed into the hut, shoving them back into the room and away from the door because she truly had no idea what was happening. All she knew was that the horse was being dragged off into the darkness, the kids were screaming, and she was terrified.

Conor, however, hadn't come into the hut; he was standing in the doorway, watching the pony as it struggled against whatever had it. It was so dark that he couldn't see whatever had the horse in its grip. Mattock was crying hysterically because his pony was being attacked and Destry found herself comforting the boy, watching Conor with a terrified expression as he watched the pony struggling in the darkness.

"What is it?" Destry asked him, her voice shaking. "Can you see anything?"

Conor's dark blue eyes were riveted to the movement in the darkness; they were over by the make-shift barn now and he could see that the pony's struggles were lessening. The animal was losing the fight. He, too, could hear the growling and snorting, as something horrific and terrible was lingering viciously in the shadows. As he opened his mouth, Padraigan suddenly appeared, rushing at him from the direction of the crude corral. She had a flaming torch in her hand, dragging something with her. She rushed at Conor, struggling with both the weight of the torch and the weight of whatever she was dragging.

"My lord," she said breathlessly. "Your weapon."

Conor looked surprised. "Weapon?" he repeated. "What...?"

Padraigan tried to lift it but she wasn't strong enough, not with one arm. Conor saw her struggles and instinctively took it from her. The little sorceress held the torch high in the direction of the struggling pony.

"I will blind it with the light," she hissed at him. "You must kill it."

"Kill what?" he demanded, frustrated and scared. "I can't even see it."

"You must, my lord," Padraigan was issuing a command. "Kill it now!"

Conor's gaze lingered on the woman before taking a look at the weapon he now held in his hand; it was heavy and as he lifted it up, into the light, he could see that it was a gloriously crafted broadsword. The magnificent piece was massive, at least four feet long, with a thick, sharp blade etched with Celtic crosses and other Celtic designs. The hilt was forged from a solid piece of steel and as he put his hand around the leather pommel, he realized that it fit his grip perfectly. He was quickly becoming enamored with the beauty and craftsmanship of the blade until Padraigan hissed at him again.

"My lord!" she beckoned him, motioning for him to follow her. "We must kill it because it will come for us when it finishes with the pony. Hurry!"

Conor didn't like the sound of that at all but he still couldn't see what had the horse. "What is it?"

Padraigan's features were filled with anxiety. "Uafásach."

His brow furrowed. "Terror? What terror?"

"Please," Padraigan urged. "You are a great warrior, my lord. You have killed many *fiacla nathair*. Hurry!"

Snake teeth, Conor translated to himself. It sounded too weird, too bizarre to adequately comprehend. But he was urged on simply by the woman's words and the pony's screaming. He could no longer stand by idle. He glanced at Destry before he charged on, seeing fear and trust in her eyes, and it fed him like nothing else he had ever known. As Padraigan ran towards the barn with the torch held high, he charged after her.

He could see the pony in the darkness, lying on its side as something chomped on its leg. Conor was a man trained the art of medieval warfare; he'd trained seven years' worth of students in the same thing and considered himself an expert. He knew tactics, weapons and psychology. But nothing prepared him for the sight of the night creature when his gaze finally beheld it; Padraigan rushed forward with the torch and the thing screamed, releasing the pony and recoiling back in fear of the fire. Conor could see that it was some kind of enormous lizard with great jagged teeth - he couldn't have described it any other way. But it was horrifying, like something out of a bad horror movie, and for a moment he was actually stunned into inaction. As Padraigan thrust the torch at it, Conor just stood there with his jaw slack, drinking in something he could have never imagined in his wildest dreams.

But he was spurred into action by Padraigan's howl when the beast suddenly reared back and spit at her. Something horrible smelling and steamy hit the ground, scorching all it touched.

"I will distract it, my lord!" Padraigan called to him, her voice tense. "Kill it!"

Conor could feel his heart pounding in his chest, both terrified and strangely excited. This was something new, horrifying and weirdly brilliant. He was in the middle of something he couldn't quite comprehend, like a dream, but in spite of that he knew what he had to do. He needed to call upon his classical weapons training and carve into a beast he'd never even heard of much less seen. He had no idea what it was but he knew he had to kill it. He couldn't chance that the thing would go after Destry or the children; he was the only defense they had and he was going to kill it before it killed them.

He took a deep breath and cleared his mind, thinking logically on how to approach the hissing creature as Padraigan bravely thrust the torch at it, using the fire to distract it. But as Conor got a good grip on the enormous broadsword and circled off to the left of the animal, moving out of its line of sight, he could hear Padraigan uttering faint, mysterious words.

"A gheobhaidh tú ar ais leis an dorchadas," she hissed. *"Chréatúr de, fiacla olc dubh an bháis, ar ais chuig an dorchadais ó áit a tháinig tú."*

She's casting a spell, Conor thought as he moved with stealth to the left, translating Padraigan's words as he went, to the darkness you will return, creature of evil, black teeth of death, return to the darkness from where you came. It all seemed surreal as he got a good look at the animal, something scaly and prehistoric-looking. He couldn't even be clinical as he studied it; this thing went beyond what his scientific mind was capable of analyzing. He tightened his grip on the sword, watching the thing spit some kind of secretion that sizzled and burned at the foliage beneath its feet. It was horrible and terrifying. And he could waste no more time.

He charged forward, holding the blade aloft in both hands as he aimed for the torso were the front legs joined with the chest. He fell upon the cold and scaly beast, ramming the sword into its body as hard as he could.

The creature screamed, sounding very much like a human cry, and fell over onto its left side. Conor withdrew the sword and plunged it in again and again. As the beast went through its death throes, a claw caught Conor on the right shoulder blade and he fell back, rolling away from the creature that was thrashing about violently. Somehow, he ended up about twenty feet away, watching the beast die. He didn't even remember how he got there. He just stood there and watched the animal as its thrashing grew less and less until finally, the beast gave one huge shudder and suddenly lay still.

The air was abruptly quiet, the only sounds those of distant night birds or an occasional forest creature. It was so oddly and instantly still that Conor felt as if he couldn't breathe. It was as if the silence had sucked the air right out of his lungs. When he finally resumed breathing, it sounded as if he was gasping. He just couldn't believe what had happened, what he had done, but the proof was dead and bleeding in front of him.

Padraigan leaned over the beast, jabbing it with her torch to make sure it was dead. As Conor stood there, stunned, she turned to the pony, who was still on the ground with a mauled rear leg. The pony nickered softly in pain and Padraigan called to Conor.

"My lord," she said, her voice quivering from the stress and fear she had so recently endured. "The pony is injured. You must ease him into the next world."

Conor was still staring at the dead beast but he managed to get his legs moving and made his way over to the little white pony. By this time, Destry and the boys had spilled out from the cottage, timidly making their way towards Conor and the dead creature. Destry had Slane by the hand but Mattock broke loose and ran to his pony. When he saw the state of the animal's leg, the tears began to flow.

"Deneb," he fell to his knees, stroking the soft white fur. "'Twill be all right, boy."

Conor stood over the pony, seeing the mangled leg and knowing that it was unsalvageable. His heart went out to the boy as Destry walked up beside him. Her soft, warm hand touched his wrist.

"Are you all right?" she whispered.

He nodded, still staring at the boy. "I'm fine."

"What in the hell was that?"

Conor tore his focus away from the pony and looked down at her. He suddenly very much wanted to feel her in his arms, her reassuring warmth and softness, so he put his big arms around her and held her tightly. Suddenly, he felt shaken and frightened, now that it was all over, looking to Destry as his source of strength. He really needed to hold her, just for a moment. He'd never been so scared in his entire life.

Destry could feel him shaking and she let go of Slane's hand, putting her arms around Conor and hugging him tightly. He really seemed shook up and she found herself in the role of giving comfort.

"It's all right," she murmured to him, her hands caressing his broad back. "It's all over now. Everything is all right."

He just stood there and trembled. Destry unwound her arms from his waist and pulled back to look him in the face, her hands going to his cheeks. She looked him in the eye.

"Do you hear me?" she whispered, smiling encouragingly. "It's all over and you did fine. We're all fine."

He just looked at her, his pale face even paler. He couldn't even speak. Clucking with sympathy, she threw her arms around his neck and kissed his cheeks, whispering words of comfort. As Conor wrapped her up in his enormous arms again, they heard soft sobs off to the left and turned to see Mattock weeping quietly over his pony. The boy was broken up and Conor wasn't so shaken that he didn't know what needed to be done. Taking a deep breath, he steadied himself and scrambled to bring his wits about him.

"Take the boys inside," he told Destry. "I need to... take care of the pony."

Destry looked up at him with her bright blue eyes. "What are you going to do?"

He just looked at her and she got the hint. "Just... take them inside," he said softly.

Destry let go of Conor and went to Mattock, timidly putting her hands on the boy's shoulders. The lad began to weep harder when he realized that they were trying to separate him from his beloved pony.

"Conor," Destry looked up at him, desperate. "I don't speak his language. Tell him to come with me."

Conor leaned over, putting his enormous hand on the boy's auburn head. "Mattock," he said in Gaelic. "Go with... with your mother. Go inside now."

Mattock shook his head, weeping pitifully. Destry felt so sorry for the boy; she hugged him gently, trying to pull him away from the pony.

"How can I tell him that everything will be okay?" she asked Conor.

Conor helped her pull the boy up. *"Beidh gach rud ceart go leor."*

Destry put her arms around the child, her head against his. *"Beidh gach rud ceart go leor,"* she repeated softly. "Everything will be all right, Mattock. Come inside."

She managed to pull him away from the bleeding animal. Conor took hold of Devlin and Slane, directing them to follow. He stood there and watched as Destry escorted the boys back inside the mud hut, his gaze lingering on the gently glowing open door even after they had disappeared through it. It had been an extremely eventful night in a day that had been full of such monumental events and he still wasn't quite sure how he felt about it. But he was glad for one thing; Destry was with him. All of the craziness and bizarre happenings aside, he could handle anything that was thrown at him as long as she was with him.

He sighed faintly, turning back to the dead creature several feet away with the sword still stuck in its belly. Conor went to retrieve the sword, feeling a little squeamish about what he needed to do with the pony. He went to the little horse, gazing down into its big brown eyes as Padraigan began to throw wood all around the dead beast. As Conor reluctantly took care of the horse, Padraigan made a neat bonfire around the lizardy beast and lit it with the torch in her hand.

With the inky darkness surrounding them, Conor went to stand next to Padraigan as she murmuring spells into the night that would cast the creature's soul deep into the underworld. As an anthropologist, he found it extremely interesting and curious, but as a man who had just killed some kind of mythical beast, he was willing to believe that that science wasn't all it was cracked up to be. Maybe a little magic was something to put some faith in.

CHAPTER NINE

By the time Conor and Padraigan entered the hut, the fire was burning low in the hearth and everything was still and quiet. Poking his head into the smaller room that contained the small bed, he found Destry and the boys asleep.

"Eat something, my lord," Padraigan whispered, indicating he sit at the table.

Conor was exhausted but he realized he was also very hungry. With everything that had happened, it didn't even occur to him until now. So he pulled up one of those little stools and sat heavily, watching Padraigan bring bread, cheese and a big steaming bowl of something to the table. She had dished it out from a big iron pot that sat tucked back in the hearth and he smelled it suspiciously, trying to figure out what it was.

Padraigan watched him anxiously. "Is it not to your satisfaction, my lord?"

He half-shrugged, half-nodded. "What is it?"

"Fowl," she told him. "It is cooked with grains and greens."

Conor figured he had nothing to lose by trying it. He tore apart a big hunk of the rustic bread, very brown, and dipped it into the stew. He didn't plan on it being delicious. It was basically a thick chicken and barley stew with peas and something white, which he thought might be turnips. He couldn't really tell. But it was hearty and tasty, and very salty, and he ended up eating about a half-gallon of the stuff. Padraigan also produced boiled eggs, smaller and denser than modern eggs, and he ate a dozen of those as well. Along with the loaf of dark bread and half-pound of cheese, Conor had polished off a significant meal. He washed it all down with a very tart wine that gave him a pretty decent buzz.

Exhausted, full, he sat at the table and burped as Padraigan cleared away the remainders of his meal.

"Go and sleep tonight, my lord," she told him, pointing to the room where Destry and the boys were. "We will speak again in the morning."

Conor didn't argue; his mind was muddled and he couldn't think any longer. He just wanted to sleep for a while and forget all of this madness. Maybe it would all be gone when he woke up in the morning; but as he rose from the stool and stood in the doorway of the smaller bed chamber, he sincerely wished that he wasn't dreaming. He didn't want to wake up and find Destry a figment of his imagination.

It was dark in the room but he could see the layout of the group; Destry was on the bed with the mattress of leaves and branches, sleeping on her left side and turned away from him. Mattock was curled up at her feet while Slane and Devlin were sleeping on her left. She was lying so that her right arm was around both boys, protectively. Conor stood there a moment, watching the tender scene, feeling warmth and contentment in his veins. What was it Destry had said to him? *I know my children.* Apparently, she did. It was obvious in everything about her. He knew his children, too. And he also knew his wife.

He was dressed in jeans and the heavy shirt and jacket. He quietly pulled the jacket off, laying it on the ground near the bed, and pulled off the shirt as well. It landed on top of the jacket. Lowering himself to the floor, he removed his shoes, his socks, and finally his belt. They all ended up with the jacket and shirt. Quietly, he lay down beside Destry in a moment he would remember for the rest of his life.

She had taken off the jacket and sweater she had been wearing earlier, clad only in her jeans and a light weight, long sleeved shirt. The moment he lay down next to her, she took her arm off the boys and turned around to face him. Conor wrapped his enormous arms around her and pulled her close against his naked chest. He could feel her face against his skin, her breath hot on his chest, and his physical reaction was almost instantaneous. He wanted to bury himself in her softness and never let go. He pulled her closer.

"Are you sure you're okay after all of that?" Destry whispered.

"I'm fine," he murmured.

She pulled her face out of his chest and gazed up at him in the muted light. "I saw that scratch on your back," she whispered. "I should probably take a look at it."

He looked into her sleepy face, wanting very much to kiss her. He was buzzed from the wine, that was true, but his feelings for her had nothing to do with alcohol. He was in love with her; he'd always been in love with her. It was something that grew stronger by the minute.

"It's nothing," he assured her. "I can't even feel it. You can look at it in the morning if it'll make you happy."

"You don't know for sure that it's nothing," she countered. "What the hell was that thing, anyway?"

He shook his head. "I have no idea," he said. "Padraigan called it a snake with teeth. It looked like something prehistoric to me."

Destry's bright blue eyes were fixed on him. There was fear in her expression. "Is that even possible?" she wanted to know. "A dinosaur?"

He shrugged. "Legends abound from this time in history," he murmured, his hands caressing her back, feeling the texture of her hair.

"There were all sorts of legends of creatures. It's possible that there was some basis for that, creatures that somehow survived millions of years only to be made extinct by Dark Age Man."

She pursed her lips wryly. "You saw the proof with your own eyes," she hissed. "You killed the damn thing. What if there are more of them?"

He sighed faintly. "Then I'll be killing a lot of lizards, I suppose," he winked at her when she frowned. "Right now, I don't want to think about it. I just want to sleep."

She let him pull her back against him, cuddled up against his enormous chest. But her eyes were open, staring into the darkness as she felt his warmth wrap all around her.

"Do we even know what time period this is?" she asked softly. "Did you ask the sorceress?"

She felt him sigh. "I asked her a few questions and was able to determine that Gofraid is the king of Dublin right now."

"When did he reign?"

"He ruled from 934 A.D. to 941 A.D., so we're somewhere in that time span, I would guess."

She lifted her head again, looking at him with shock. "Then we're really here. We actually went back in time somehow."

He focused his dark blue eyes on her. "After what I've seen today, I would agree with that statement."

"Are you scared?"

He shrugged. "I think I'm curious more than anything. But that big snake with teeth... that thing scared me."

"Me, too."

Hearing that somehow brought it all home for Destry. Whatever had happened to them was as real as it gets. Somehow, someway, a door in time opened up and they stepped through it. It was fantastic to the point of being insane but she knew it was the truth. There was no other explanation. Frightened and exhausted herself, she closed her eyes and fell back against him.

Conor knew she was upset. He wrapped his enormous arms around her, his lips against her forehead, kissing her gently to bring her some comfort. To his surprise, she lifted her mouth to him and he latched onto her hungrily. As her arms went around his neck, he rolled her onto her back and kissed her deeply.

She responded to him strongly. With every second that passed, his kiss became more heated and he licked at her lips, his tongue tasting her sweetness when she opened her mouth and invited him in. Her fingers where in his hair, still spiked stiff, matching him suckle for suckle as his right hand moved down her torso and found a full breast. She had such a delicious little body that he just couldn't help himself.

Rather than flinch from his touch, she lifted up her shirt and unhooked her bra at the front. Conor's hand came into contact with the heated flesh of her naked breast and he groaned softly in excitement, feeling the nipple harden in his palm.   He was trying to stay quiet; God help him, he was desperately trying. There was a four year old and an eight year old just a few feet away and he didn't want to wake them. But he couldn't stop himself from exploring Destry, something that was becoming less like exploration and more like reacquainting. Even as he fondled her soft breasts, it was as if he already knew their texture and softness. He already knew her body. He had to taste her.

His hot mouth went to a nipple and Destry had to slap her hand over her mouth to keep from making noise. As Conor furiously suckled, Slane suddenly moved in his sleep, rolling into his brother and sending them both sliding off the bedding. The boys ended up in a little heap on the floor, still half-way on the blanket, and Conor and Destry froze, watching to see if they'd wake up. But both boys were sleeping so heavily that they weren't even aware of the fact that they had rolled right off the bed. Conor grinned at Destry, who merely wriggled her eyebrows. Then she latched on to Conor's mouth and kissed him hotly.

Their passion took flight and clothes began coming off in the darkness, kisses and passionate touches between them. Connor left her breasts and yanked off her jeans, planting himself between her legs as his mouth worked across her flat belly. The smell of her, the taste of her, was feeding his frenzy and his right hand left her breasts to move to the junction between her legs. So far, she wasn't flinching from his touch and in fact seemed to be encouraging him. He could feel her squirming beneath his body and it excited him like nothing he had ever known. When his hand reached her inner thigh and he realized that her pubic area was completely waxed, he audibly groaned with excitement.

"Shhh," Destry whispered, her hand over his mouth.

Conor kissed her fingers, one by one, before descending on the pink folds between her legs. Destry's knees came up at the delicious sensation and a moan escaped her lips.

"Shhh," Conor grinned as he put a big hand over her mouth.

She rewarded him by sucking on his fingers, her tongue stroking his index finger as he performed oral sex on her. Driven beyond endurance by her heated tongue and sexy body, Conor sat back on his heels and lifted Destry onto his waiting erection. He didn't want to grind her tender back into the rough mattress so he sat on his heels while she straddled his lap. As the boys around them slept like the dead, Destry wrapped her arms around his neck, straddled his thighs, and gave herself over to him completely.

The scent of their lovemaking stirred strong, buried memories. She began to recall innumerable nights like this, wrapped around the man she loved, feeling his power deep within her. She began to recall the depth of her feelings for the man, the love and adoration she felt for him that was more powerful than anything that had ever existed. Her soft mouth found his, feeling his goatee scratch her tender lips but loving the sensation. She kissed him deeply as he thrust into her, knowing that, at last, she was finally where she belonged.

"Oh, Conor," she breathed into his mouth. "I love you so much."

His arms tightened around her. "I've never loved anyone else but you, sweetheart," he murmured against her lips. "You are my heart and soul. I will always love you, in this life or the next."

They made love deep into the night.

***

The next day, Conor awoke at daybreak because he heard Padraigan moving around in the great room.

He blinked his eyes, struggling to orient himself because he didn't recognize where he was at first. He didn't recognize the mud walls or sloping roof. But he quickly realized that Destry was in his arms, sleeping the sleep of the dead pressed up against his warm body, and the events from the previous day and night flooded his mind. He remembered Dowth, the flight to Padraigan's hut, the snake with teeth... everything.

Most of all, he remembered the feel of Destry and his limbs grew warm at the thought. He'd never known anything so passionate, satisfying or erotic. It was as if he was finally and completely whole. As long as she was with him, as long as he had her love, he could move mountains.

Another thing he quickly realized was that they were both quite naked. He felt rather bold and caddish having made love to her in the presence of sleeping children, but there wasn't much he could do about that in hindsight so he carefully disengaged himself from her with the intention of looking for his pants. But she groaned when he moved and he put a hand over her mouth, silencing her when she opened her eyes.

"Shhhh," he whispered, kissing her nose. "The boys are still asleep."

She was still half-asleep. "Where are you going?"

He kissed her again and slowly moved to sit up. "I need to find my clothes," he whispered, spying his jeans next to the bed. "I'm without a stitch on. And so are you. If the boys wake up and find us like this, we'll have a lot of explaining to do."

Destry blinked, rubbing her eyes as she looked around. The boys were still dead asleep but she realized that Conor was correct; she was stark naked. She sat up, her arms covering her substantial breasts.

"Oh, brother," she hissed. "Where are my clothes?"

Conor was fighting off a grin as she tried to cover herself up. But her DD cup breasts could hardly be contained by her slender arms and he lost himself for a moment, burying his face in the delightful cleavage. She gasped, giggled, then groaned softly as he moved her right arm aside and suckled gently on a peaked nipple.

"Conor, don't," she gasped, her face in the top of his head.

He lifted his head, kissing her lips as his fingers played with the nipple. "I'm sorry," he whispered. "I got carried away. You seem to have that effect on me."

She grinned at him, quickly feeling hot and horny as he played with her nipple. It wasn't so much a want for the man but a need; she needed the man more than she could comprehend. Her body was crying out for him, having been denied for the months and years and centuries of their separation and last night evidenced that.

 Now that she had re-acquainted herself with him, fragments of memories about the man and her love for him returning, she had to make up for lost time. Her lips slanted over his, her tongue plunging into his mouth, and Conor fell back on the bed, taking her down with him. This time, however, she climbed on top of him, straddling his belly as she ferociously kissed him.

Conor could feel her naked body against him, her wet heat rubbing against his belly, and it was all he could take. He was intoxicated with her, his hands cupping her buttocks as his fingers probed intimate places. When he thrust a finger into her, she groaned into his mouth and pushed her pelvis against his finger, simulating intercourse. Conor groaned softly in return, as wildly aroused as he had ever been in his life, as he lifted her up and planted her onto his full-engorged erection. He could feel her warm tightness as she slid down over him, accepting his sensual intrusion into her body.

Destry drew away from his mouth as she sat up, taking his hands and placing them on her breasts as she began to ride him. Knees on the ground, she rolled her hips forward and plunged down on him again and again as he fondled her breasts, her head back and her long hair tickling the tops of his thighs. Twice, she started to groan and twice, Conor put his hand up to gently cover her mouth, reminding her that they didn't want to attract any attention. What they were doing was between the two of them, her supple and shapely body welcoming his power deep inside her as it had so many times before, in so many forms. At the moment, there was only the two of them, re-experiencing something they had both sorely missed. It was a rebirth.

Destry plunged down on him, again and again, hearing the man hiss with the pleasure of it. Conor watched her as she made love to him, marveling at her beauty and perfection, before sitting up and pulling her against him, suckling her nipples as she continued to ride him. Destry was so highly aroused that in little time, she was climaxing, wave after wave of pleasure rushing over her as Conor repeatedly thrust himself deep.

He felt her orgasm throbbing around him and he answered by releasing himself deep into her body, taking so much pleasure with it that he bit his lip in his ecstasy. He could taste the blood. But he still continued to move, feeling her multiple orgasms that ended up reducing her to a quivering shell in his arms. Her entire body was throbbing against him and his mouth moved slowly, deliciously, over her neck and shoulder as the tremors eventually died away.

Destry remained straddled on his lap, weak and limp, as he held her close. He could feel her heart thumping against him. Her hair was in her face, all over his shoulder, and as he loosened his grip, she lolled back. Her head rolled back as well and Conor grinned as she remained lifeless and boneless in his arms. He leaned forward as she listed back, kissing her neck, the swell of her breasts, and eventually a soft nipple. When he suckled her tenderly, her head came up.

"No," she whispered, her hands pulling his head back. "Not again. We really should get dressed before these kids wake up and catch us."

He grinned up into her half-lidded face. "I'd rather do this."

She grinned in return, a delightfully sleepy gesture. "Me, too," she whispered, "but we're going to have to wait for more privacy. We've already risked being caught twice and I really feel dirty having done this in front of these kids, but...."

They had let their lust get the better of them and they both knew it, but there was something so overwhelming about feelings they were awakening that it seemed to supersede all else. Conor sighed in agreement, in disappointment, realizing their bodies were still fused and lifting Destry up by the waist to withdraw from her. But the moment he did so, another orgasm washed over her and she threw her head forward, biting off her cries on his shoulder as a powerful climaxed surged through her body. It was unexpected and deliriously sweet. Her teeth pushed into his pale flesh, leaving a mark.

Conor couldn't control himself and he lowered her back down onto his semi-erection, grinding his pelvis against her as he greedily soaked up the last few tremors of her orgasm. Breathlessly, Destry tried to stop him but she couldn't quite get the words out of her mouth in time before he withdrew from her again and caused yet another orgasm. Her face ended up in his shoulder again as she struggled not to scream, but when Conor went to put her on his erection again, she stopped him. Instead, she grabbed his fingers and put them against her vagina. Conor thrust a few fingers inside of her, his thumb on her clitoris, rubbing her gently and easing her off of a series of very powerful orgasms. It was like nothing else either one of them had ever experienced, something magical and emotional that fed the physical need.

When the ripples finally died away and Conor withdrew his fingers, he held her tightly against him, kissing her neck and mussed hair.

"Are you okay?" he whispered.

Destry nodded weakly. "Uh-huh."

"Can we get dressed now?"

She lifted her head wearily, smiling. "What's stopping you?"

"You are."

"Complaining?"

"God, no," he rubbed his nose tenderly against hers. His blue eyes locked with her bright blue ones and, for a moment, they just stared at each other. "Any regrets?"

She shook her head. "No," she whispered. "Absolutely not."

"You're sure?"

"Yes."

"Good." He pulled back to look at her, his dark blue eyes intense with emotion. "Because I love you. I'll love you until I die."

She smiled, a soft hand going to his rough cheek. "I love you, too."

He stared at her, a smile eventually coming to his lips. "I know it doesn't make any sense, but nothing has ever felt so right. The moment I saw you I knew I loved you. I've always loved you."

She leaned forward, kissing him sweetly. "It's so strange," she said as she pulled away. "Pieces of memories are coming back to me but I really can't figure out if it's because I'm imagining them or because they're truly memories from some past life. But the memory of you… it came back so strongly last night. The moment you touched me, I remembered you. I remembered everything and now I can't seem to let you go."

He nodded faintly. "I know what you mean," he whispered. "The second I touched you, everything came flooding back. Your taste, your scent, your curves… everything."

She smiled at him, her hand on his cheek, rubbing his stubble as she gazed at his face. He was such a handsome man. But before she could say anything more, Padraigan suddenly entered the small doorway, her arms full of clothing. Unimpressed by Conor and Destry's naked state and the fact that Destry was still straddling Conor's lap, the little sorceress went to the bed and dumped the pile.

"Your clothing, my lord," she turned to the pair. "I managed to salvage some of it when Geric confiscated the castle. I have these possessions and more. After you dress, I shall show you."

Destry was wrapped up in Conor's enormous arms so she wasn't entirely exposed, and Conor was sideways so he wasn't providing a completely naughty display, but they were both very uncomfortable with an audience to their nakedness. More than that, it was readily apparent what they had been doing. If Padraigan had been in the next room or even the next county, she would have easily heard them. But the sorceress seemed unconcerned. She rummaged through the pile and pulled out some kind of white robe. She turned and held it out to Destry.

"My lady?" she said. "May I assist you?"

Destry didn't have a clue what the woman was saying. She looked to Conor for help and he took pity on her; at least he could understand what was being said, but Destry had no recollection or knowledge of a former language. It must have made the situation particularly disorienting but, so far, she hadn't complained about the communication barrier in the least.

"She wants to know if she can help you dress," he told her.

Destry lifted a reluctant eyebrow. "I don't think so," she said. "Thank her but tell her that I'll dress alone."

Conor relayed the words and Padraigan lay the robe back on the bed and quit the room. When the woman was gone, Destry jumped up and went for her bra and panties, which were in a silky pile next to the bed.

Conor watched with great appreciation and admiration as she slipped on her lacy panties followed by the lacy white bra. She had a fabulous body, the most beautiful he had ever seen. His hungry gaze moved up her silky thighs, lingered on the lacy panties, before moving up her torso to her full breasts. He was thinking very dirty thoughts again as she bent over and picked up her jeans. He stopped her.

"Wait," he said quietly. "If we're going to be stuck in this time, the last thing we want to do is stand out. We need to blend in and that's not going to happen if you wear those jeans."

She looked at the jeans in her hand, nodding her head when he realized he made some sense. Her gaze moved to the flowing white robe that Padraigan had lain upon the bed. Jeans still in hand, she moved over to the garment and observed it with some fear.

"All right," she sighed heavily as she folded the jeans up and set them aside. She picked up the white robe, realizing it was like a giant flowing muumuu. She further realized that it was very soft and she rubbed it against her cheek, looking at Conor with a grin. "It's soft. I think I can wear this."

He smiled back, his gaze once again trailing down the curve of her back and coming to rest on her delicious buttocks. He just couldn't help himself. His big hand came up, stroking her rounded butt cheek, squeezing it, before bending over to nibble at it. Destry giggled and pulled away from him.

"Come on," she said reproachfully. "If you keep doing that, we'll never get dressed."

He wriggled his eyebrows at her in resignation and stood up. Destry burst into snorts of laughter when she saw that he was semi-aroused again. He pursed his lips with mock-fury as she laughed.

"It's not funny," he told her.

She continued to giggle softly as she pulled the dress over her head, immediately loving the feel and fit of it. It clung to her beautifully, as if made for her. As Destry smoothed at the garment, she realized that it had been made for her. The fit was perfect. Running her hands up and down the arms, noting the softness of the fabric, she glanced over to see Conor examining the leather pants that Padraigan had left on the end of the bed. He had pulled his boxer-briefs on so he wasn't completely nude as he stood inspecting the stitching on the inseam of the pants. Curious, Destry went to see what had him so fascinated.

"What's wrong?" she asked.

He shook his head, riveted to the stitching. "Nothing," he said. "I was just looking at the craftsmanship on these breeches. The leather is sewn together with very fine strips of leather. It's really remarkable."

Destry tried hard to see what he was looking at but, not being a scientist like he was, it really didn't mean all that much to her. So she bent over the end of the bed where Padraigan had laid the pile of garments and began pulling out various garments. There was a long, dark green article of clothing that looked like a robe, a faded yellow one with beautiful beadwork around the neckline, and several others. She ran her hands over the material, seeing that it wasn't like any material she had ever seen in her life. The green garment was made from wool, very fine, but the weave was uneven. The yellow garment was silk, she was sure, but it was also uneven and the color wasn't uniform. Everything was stitched with tiny hand-stitches and the hems of the garments weren't sewn at all but all things considered, they seem to be very well made.

As Conor pulled on the leather pants, Destry took the long, green robe and put it on over the feather-soft dress she already had on. She was delighted to see that the long sleeves on the green garment had slits in them, allowing the eggshell-colored dress underneath to show through.

The green robe also had a belt with fine tassels on the end and she tied it around her waist, emphasizing her slender torso and very large breasts. By the time Conor looked up from lacing the front of his leather pants up, the sight of her in the flowing robes made his heart leap in all directions.

"My God," he breathed. "You're a lovely creature."

She was fussing with the tassels, looking up with a grin when he spoke. "Thanks," she said. "I really have no idea if these are even supposed to go together but they seem to. Am I wearing it right?"

He looked her over with his critical Celtic eye, having her spin a circle for him. He nodded with satisfaction.

"There has never been another woman on this earth as beautiful as you," he said decisively. "You're spectacular."

Her grin broadened modestly. "You're sweet; thank you," she said, and her grin faded. "I'd love to shower and shave right now, but I'm guessing that's not going to be possible."

He shrugged, tugging at the leather breeches as he reached down into the pile on the bed and began hunting for a shirt of some kind.

"Probably not," he replied. He found a woolen shirt, or what he thought was a woolen shirt big enough to fit his frame, and pulled it over his head. "There's a whole host of things we need and don't have. I need to talk to Padraigan to see where we can at least get soap and basic hygiene needs. What we can't buy, I can make."

Her eyebrows lifted. "What can you make?"

He shrugged again, straightening out the tunic. Destry moved forward to help him straighten out the back of it, smoothing the tunic against his very broad back.

"A toothbrush, for example," he said. "They were made out of water reeds or green branches, something that frayed easily. We can make toothpaste out of soda and mint, all mashed together. Soap can be made from any number of oils that occur naturally and lye, or lotions from almond oil or beeswax. I promise that you'll not do without, sweetheart. We'll keep your skin soft and your smile bright."

Her smile was back. "You can make all of that? Where did you learn to do it?"

He returned her smile. "Back in the early days when I was still going to college, I worked several medieval fairs all around Ireland. Since I'm such a big fella, I was always some kind of warrior but during those years but I learned a lot about ancient processes with food and other things. I learned how to make soap, candles, certain medicines, things like that. It's come in very handy to pass down to my students. I'm a walking dictionary for all things ancient."

She sighed. "If I have to be stranded in the past with someone, thank God it's you," she said, watching him wink at her. "I have to tell you that I'm still feeling a little disoriented. What's our first plan of attack for this morning?"

Conor eyed the boots that Padraigan had dropped at the foot of the bed, massive things made from cow hide. He picked one up and began to inspect it.

"I'm not sure," he told her. "I need to talk to the sorceress and try to figure some things out. Meanwhile, you can get the boys up and ready for breakfast."

He was nodding his head towards the boys. Destry turned to see that they were just starting to stir. Little mouths were yawning. She shook her head, grinning.

"Now they wake up," she commented softly. "We made so much noise last night and this morning that it would have awoken the dead, but those three slept right through it."

Conor fought off a grin. "Thank God they didn't wake up," he muttered. "We didn't need an audience for what we were doing but I'm not sure I would have been able to stop had they woken up, so I'll thank God for small mercies. The lads can sleep through anything."

Destry was grinning because he was and went to pull on her shoes, fancy modern sneakers with straps and rhinestones.

"I never grew up with brothers so I can't attest to boys' ability to sleep through anything, but I know my sister and I were very light sleepers," she told him as she slipped on a shoe. "We heard every little sound in the house."

Conor pulled on both boots, inspecting them on his feet and realizing they were a perfect fit. "I'll be damned," he muttered, running his hand over the sole of the shoe. "These fit as if...."

He trailed off and she sat down next to him on the foot of the bed, looking at the shoes on his feet. "As if they were made for you?"

Her voice was soft and he looked over at her, feeling the weight of their situation settle where he had been fairly detached from it since they had woken up. For some reason, the boots seemed to bring it home. If he thought hard about them, he thought he might remember them somehow, like a distant dream just lingering below the surface. Gazing into her bright blue eyes, he nodded with some reluctance.

"Yes," he murmured. "This just keeps getting weirder and weirder. These shoes fit perfectly."

"And you're surprised?"

He wriggled his red eyebrows. "It's not that," he sighed. "I guess... I guess I'm just not as resigned to all of this as much as I thought."

"Why?"

He shrugged. "It's all so overwhelming. Just when I think I've accepted it, something happens and I realize I really haven't."

"Like Dark Ages boots that were made for you?"

"Yes."

She gave him a sweet smile and laid her head against his enormous shoulder. "Don't go to pieces on me now," she said softly. "I can't guarantee how I'm going to hold up if you don't stay strong."

He shifted, wrapping his enormous arms around her and pulling her close. He kissed the tip of her nose, her soft mouth. She was soft and delicious, and he was in the process of kissing her more deeply when Slane suddenly groaned, a grumpy little sound, and sat bolt up-right. He rubbed his eyes, frowning when he saw Destry and Conor in a tight embrace. As they watched, he stood up, eyes still half closed and a frown on his face, and wedged himself in between them.

Destry giggled as Conor was forced to let her go as the four-year-old plastered himself against her. She wrapped her arms around the little boy as he snuggled against her and promptly fell back asleep. Conor just shook his head and stood up, feeling the fit of the boots and clothing, acquainting himself with something that felt oddly familiar.

Padraigan entered the room again, this time with a bucket of water, which she handed to Conor. He took it, having no idea what to do with it, but set it on the broad windowsill as Padraigan moved to Mattock and Devlin, still sleeping on the floor. She shook Mattock by the shoulder before doing the same to Devlin. The boys groaned and stirred, rubbing their eyes and sitting up from a deep sleep.

Mattock blinked his eyes when he saw his father standing there in familiar clothing. His young face lit up with delight as Devlin, catching sight of the same vision, jumped up and ran to Conor, throwing his arms around the man's waist.

"Dada," the boy nearly wept. "You're really here. I thought I'd dreamed you."

Mattock joined his brother, his face shining up at Conor adoringly. "Dada, will you ride with us today?" he asked.

Conor had one hand on Devlin and the other on Mattock, smiling at boys that he was increasingly convinced he fathered.

 Like last night, the memories were coming back to him in pieces but he knew for certain that they were recollections and not his imagination. The feelings associated with them, the emotion, were far too strong to be anything else.

"Ride with you?" he repeated, turning to look at Padraigan. "What does he mean?"

Padraigan smiled as she crouched on the floor, rolling up the bedding. "You would take your boys riding with you every morning, my lord," she explained. "You would go about your duties, checking posts and meeting with your generals, and bring the boys. You said it was important for them to understand their duties to the land as well as to the people."

By this time, Destry had stood up from the bed, the four year old still clinging to her. His little head was on her shoulder, his arms around her neck as his legs wrapped around Destry's torso. Hugging the boy, Destry made her way over to Conor and the other two.

"What are they saying?" she wanted to know.

Conor looked at her with the boy wrapped up all around her and he grinned, putting his hand on Slane's back.

"He looks like a parasite," he snorted.

Destry grinned. "He has no intention of letting me go."

Conor's eyes glimmered at her. "Neither do I," he winked at her, glancing back at Devlin and Mattock. "In answer to your question, the boys wanted to know if I was going to take them riding. Padraigan said that it was something I would do with them every morning because I told them it was important for them to understand their duties to the land as well as to the people."

Destry's expression turned warm. "That sounds like something you would say. Call it a hunch, Conor, but I would guess that you were a pretty amazing king."

His smile grew, appreciative, prevented from answering her as the boys began to clamor around him, grabbing his hands and pulling him from the small chamber. Destry followed with Slane still clinging to her, pausing in the open doorway, as Padraigan followed them out into the yard.

"You cannot ride, my lord," she told him. "You would risk being seen."

Conor turned to look at her, catching a glimpse of the burnt body of the dragon-like creature over near the crude stable. In the light of the new morning, he stared at it, being reminded yet again that he had awoken to a different place and time. He drew in a long breathe, resigning himself, forcing himself to focus on the situation at hand. He had no choice. The reality was all around him.

"So what do you suggest?" he asked. "I can't hide out here the rest of my life."

Padraigan was resolute. "I shall go into town and bring back your trusted men," she told him. "They will counsel you on what has happened in Ciannachta since you have been away. Then you will know what you must do."

He nodded simply because he couldn't think of anything else to do. They just couldn't hide in the woods for the rest of their lives. If he had a kingdom to rule, and people waiting for his triumphant return, then they'd better get about it.

"All right," he waved her on. "I'll wait here."

Padraigan's pale lips met with a smile. "Your men will be very glad to know you have returned. We have waited so long for this day."

"How long?"

She didn't hesitate. "Three hundred and sixty sun rises, my lord," she told him. "We have waited a very long time."

Conor smiled because she was. Swiftly, she turned for the barn, instructing the boys on their chores while she was gone. Mattock and Devlin made unhappy faces but the begrudgingly did as they were told, going to feed the chickens and milk the fat cow. Conor stood out in the yard, watching the boys go about their duties. He could see Destry inside the doorway of the little hut, brushing her hair with her fingers as Slane, now out of her arms, followed her around by holding on to her skirt. Conor had to grin at the little boy who had no intention of letting her out of his sight.

And then, it struck him - *his family*. If he'd had any shadow of a doubt before, seeing Destry with Slane, seeing the older boys going about their chores, and listening to a white witch speak of things so natural cemented into his heart and soul that this was where he belonged. As he'd told Destry, he'd always felt out of place, a man who didn't belong in the modern world he was born into. Here he was, here and now, and all things were as they should be. He had Destry. He had his boys. He had everything. He was back where he belonged.

He turned around, holding out a hand to Destry. With Slane still clinging on to her skirts, she made her way out to Conor, taking his hand. He held it tightly, kissing it as he composed his thoughts.

"What is it?" Destry asked. He seemed distant and pensive. "What's on your mind?"

Conor grunted as he looked around. Then he sniffed the air. "Smell that?"

Destry sniffed. She shook her head. "I smell trees."

He looked at her. "Exactly," he said. "No smog, no smells of the modern world. I suppose I had my doubts about this entire situation even until a few minutes ago, but walking out here, smelling the smells and hearing the birds and wind through the trees... I'm not feeling any more doubts. As much as I knew you belonged to me the moment I met you, right now, I feel like this belongs to me, too. I belong here. Whatever has happened to us, maybe it wasn't a mistake. Like Padraigan said, maybe it really *was* magic. It was something that was meant to happen."

Destry was listening to him seriously. "I guess all things happen for a reason," she said with surprising acceptance; like him, she was coming to understand the reality of their situation. She looked down at Slane, sucking his thumb and holding her skirts, and smiled. "I told you last night that I know my children. These boys are mine and you are their father. I don't know how this happened, but I'm not going to question it. After what we've been through the past day or so, I'm willing to take a few things on faith. So now what?"

He sighed, putting his arm around her, grinning when Slane pushed his way in between them and clung to Destry's leg. "Now, we have a whole new world out there," he said softly. "Just think about it; I'm supposed to be the king. You're my queen. I've got an evil brother who's stolen my throne. I want the damn thing back."

Destry smiled at his animated speech. "I'll help you."

He looked at her, bending down to kiss the tip of her nose. "I think you already have," he said. "I wouldn't be here it if wasn't for you. You brought me back, Destry. You gave me my destiny."

She hugged him, trying not to squish the child between them. "Padraigan said that time and space couldn't keep us apart," she said quietly. "Whatever I did, I was meant to do it. We were meant to do it. But I think I'm a little afraid."

"Afraid of what?"

"Afraid for you," she said, gazing up at him. "Your brother went through a lot of trouble to separate us. He's not going to be happy to see you. These guys have swords and stuff. They're going to try to kill you."

He grinned. "I told you that I can fight with swords, feet, fists, and anything else they throw at us," he said. "You don't need to be afraid but you need to be smart. Listen to what I tell you and what the white witch tells you. I didn't find you after a thousand years only to see you taken away from me again."

Destry lifted her eyebrows in agreement. "Same goes for me," she murmured. "You have no idea what it would do to me if you were killed. God, it sounds so scary even to say that. We're facing a whole new world out there."

He kissed her forehead. "New and deadly and beautiful," he said. "We have the opportunity to shape the world, I think, or at least our little corner of it. Are you ready for it?"

Destry's gaze moved out over the green, green foliage, enormous trees reaching for the untamed sky, and the beams of light piercing their way through the canopy. There was such raw beauty to it and when she gazed up at Conor, all she could see was her past, her present, and her future.

"I'm ready," she said, laying her head on his chest as Slane begged to be picked up. "It sounds corny, but as long as we're together, I'm ready for anything."

"Me, too," he whispered. "I love you, sweetheart. Until the end of time, I will love only you."

She smiled at him, a genuine and heartfelt gesture that sent his heart fluttering. "I love you, too," she whispered.

He kissed her and picked up Slane, who wanted to go with his mother and not his father. Conor handed the boy over to Destry just as Mattock and Devlin raced over to him, explaining that they had seen something magical and wonderful over near the barn. Conor thought they mentioned a faerie of some kind but he couldn't be sure. The modern man, now ancient ruler, was ready for anything as he went to see what had his boys so excited. This was his world and he intended to master it as he'd done once before. This time, there would be no failure. He was back.

The high king had returned.

***

Part II, the novella HIGH KING, will be published in 2014 or 2015.

Visit Kathryn's website at www.kathrynleveque.com and subscribe for new release updates.